Adoringly, Edward

Adoringly, Edward

~~~~~~

SYDNEY WINWARD

This is a work of fiction. Names, characters, places, and incidents are either the product of the author's imagination or are used fictitiously, and any resemblance to actual persons living or dead, business establishments, events, or locales, is entirely coincidental.

Adoringly, Edward

COPYRIGHT © 2025 Sydney Winward

Cover art by LLewellenDesigns.com

Published by Silver Forge Books

All rights reserved. No part of this book may be used or reproduced in any manner whatsoever without written permission of the author except in the case of brief quotations embodied in critical articles or reviews.

Paperback 978-1-960461-15-5

http://www.sydneywinward.com

To all the readers who loved reading Rapunzel in their big book of fairy tales as a child like I did

BOOKS BY SYDNEY WINWARD

The Bloodborn Series
Bloodborn
Bloodbond
Bloodscourge
Bloodbane
Bloodcurse
Bloodheir

Sunlight and Shadows Series
A Breath of Sunlight
A Taste of Shadows
A Glimpse of Music
A Kiss of Embers
A Balm of Healing
A Weave of Starlight

Letters to Love Series
Yours, Sterling
Forever, Mirabelle
Always, Ivette
Charles, With Love
Adoringly, Edward

Novellas
A Wingless Hope
Through Wylder Meadows
Root Brew Float
On Silver Wings
Bloodmoon
Bloodvow
Selkie

Chapter One

She shouldn't be here.

In fact, this was the last place someone with her *glorious* bloodline, as her mother liked to call it, should find themselves considering the flowing drinks, the scandalous company, and the freedom of self expression.

But for one night, she wasn't Vivienne Winfield, daughter of the Edilann warlord, niece of the king himself, and cousin to the younger Prince Sterling. She was simply Vivi. And all she wanted was to have a good time with nothing held back.

Vivienne's stomach clenched with excitement as she stepped down from her carriage and smoothed the soft fabric of her black ball gown accentuated with red rosettes. The sleeves draped off her shoulders, and the bodice dipped low. It matched the black velvet half-mask resting over her eyes covered with red, floral lace.

She straightened her elbow-length black gloves and fixed her stare on the man allowing people into the party at the beautiful, mysterious estate. The large, black-spired structure had been abandoned for years. Or, at least, no one knew who actually owned the estate. Only that when word got out about the elusive masquerade, the event that happened once a year at different locations, she knew she had to attend.

She side-stepped on the path to avoid a carriage pulling off to the side of the road and eyed the invitations in the back pocket of a man's trousers several paces ahead of her. Invitations had been handed out personally by a man shrouded in a dark cloak, or so said a few testimonies of those who had claimed to see the mysterious personage.

To her grievance, she had not received an invitation herself.

In a quick movement, she bent her foot to the side and managed to snap the heel off her shoe, which caused her to "stumble" forward upon losing her balance. Her shriek alerted the man ahead of her, who just barely managed to catch her before she crashed into the ground.

In his momentary distraction, she slipped one of the invitations out of his back pocket and stuffed it down the sleeve of her glove.

"Forgive me!" she gasped, clutching onto the man's thin arms like a damsel in distress. "I don't know what I would have done should you not have caught me."

The man righted her and searched the ground, likely for the other half of her shoe. "Tis no trouble, milady. It's only a shame your shoe seems to have wandered off."

She patted his chest reassuringly and took him up on his offer for her to cut in line in front of him. She approached the man allowing people through the door with a rickety step when half her shoe was gone. When she presented the invitation, he nodded his head for her to enter.

Vivienne stepped into the dark ballroom with candles flickering from sconces on the walls and an enormous chandelier sparkling overhead. She inhaled a long, excited breath at the intensity of the music played by a small orchestra. Each musician dressed in black and wore masks of their own. She admired the dark, dancing gowns of women twirling around their well-dressed partners, taking in the carefree laughter, hidden identities, and absolute abandon.

"I saw that," someone said behind her, startling her into spinning around.

A man wearing a tailored black dress suit leaned casually against a gray stone pillar. A simple black mask covered the top half of his face. Black hair swept over his mask, longer in the front than in the back. And in his hand…

He twirled the missing piece of her shoe between his fingers, watching her with an air of nonchalance. Almost boredom. But she didn't miss the spark of excitement in his eyes that lived in her own.

Instead of defending herself and denying his silent accusation, she slipped her shoes off, tossed them to the side, and approached him with only stockings covering her bare feet. His intense gaze held hers throughout the entire duration of her short journey toward him. Another knot tied her stomach into a beautiful bow. The man was handsome. And she most certainly enjoyed the way he looked at her as if she were the only woman in the entire room.

She reached for her broken heel. Their fingers brushed. And it was as if a spark jolted from her fingertips, down her arm, and into her frenzied heart.

"I deserved an invitation," she said, her fingers still resting against his over the heel.

"Did you?" He leaned closer until the breath from his lips brushed against her cheek. "Because if so, you would have received one." But then he leaned back, and her breath caught at the way his mouth curved up in a grin. "However, I have no doubt the issuer of invitations would have been impressed with the way you acquired one, nonetheless."

"I had an extra!" the man from earlier cried out, his voice shoving its way through the door. "I swear! It was here in my pocket mere minutes ago."

"I sacrificed a good pair of shoes for it," she replied quietly, trying to hide her devious smile but not quite managing it, especially when an amused smirk lifted on his own lips.

Finally, he relinquished her broken heel, and she tucked it safely inside the hidden pocket of her dress, waiting to find out if he would rat her out to whomever their host might be.

He didn't.

Rather, he continued leaning a shoulder against the pillar, his attention still fixed on her. "Would you like to dance?"

Vivienne tapped a playful finger against her bottom lip. "I would love to. But with whom? No one has offered a poor girl in distress his hand for the dance floor."

Laughter escaped his mouth, and the pleasant sound alone sent a wave of flutters through her chest. She enjoyed the way his mouth curved into a smile, the way his teeth gleamed in the dim light, the way his body language exuded confidence with even the smallest movements.

"You are hardly a girl in distress. You can handle yourself just fine." He took her hand and pulled her closer until she bumped into his chest. "Dance with me."

She offered a playful, coy smile as she took his other hand and walked backward toward the dance floor, pulling him with her just as the musicians struck up another song. Only then did she realize she had not glanced away from him once since their chance meeting. She could not bring herself to look away when she found herself so taken with him.

The man took the lead, stepping into a dance as if he'd done it thousands of times.

Oh! She inhaled sharply at the realization. Just from his steps alone, she could tell he had extensive ballroom training. He was someone like her. Possibly even someone in her circle. Which intrigued her even more.

Within moments, she relaxed in his arms, following his lead around the room. They slipped by dozens more couples, the tables filled with refreshments and drinks, and twirled past the musicians, all without losing a single step. Not once did his movements falter. Not once did he squish her toes with his elegant, masterful feet.

Her heart pounded within her as she leaned closer to him until their bodies were pressed together. Her head rested on his shoulder. His fingers tightened around her waist.

"What color are your eyes?" she asked as their steps slowed, and their bodies swayed to the music. "I cannot tell in this lighting."

"Dark blue," he murmured against her hair.

How silly it seemed that she felt immensely comfortable in his presence already, as if she had known him for much longer than she had. Like coming home to a dear friend. Surely, he was someone she already knew.

"Are we already acquainted?"

A smile lifted on his lips as he shook his head. "I would have remembered you."

And then the song ended all too quickly, and the musicians started the next set. She couldn't bring herself to release him, and he made no move to do so either. Rather, he silently led her in another dance and another until her feet ached and her face hurt from smiling so much.

"Tonight is certainly a night for scandal, mysterious stranger." She laughed as she stepped closer and placed a hand on his chest. "You've danced far more dances with me than is appropriate."

"I don't want to let you go."

She lowered her voice to a husky whisper. "Then don't."

His dark blue gaze passed between her eyes for several long moments before he tightened his grip on her hand. He pulled her off the dance floor and up two flights of stairs while the music slowly faded behind them and people became scarcer. They entered a small room with a single ladder leading to a trapdoor overhead.

He climbed up first and opened the trapdoor, the hinges groaning in protest, before glancing down with an issued challenge in his eyes. A sense of thrill alighted in her heart as she gathered her masses of skirts in her arms and climbed after him.

Although she wrestled with her skirts the entire way, when she reached for the top, he gripped her hand and heaved her out the rest of the way until they stood on a small, fenced platform high above the rest of the world.

The breath faltered in her lungs at the magnificent view of the forests, the mountains, and even the Edilann palace— her home—in the distance. Lazy white clouds streaked across the dark canvas of the sky, the edges glowing silver when passing over the moon.

She spotted rows of carriages far down below while guests ambled about the garden. A light breeze scattered fallen leaves across the brick path weaving around bare trees and dormant bushes. Lanterns lit up the property like small specks of starlight, creating a mysterious yet intriguing atmosphere.

Mysterious and intriguing…just like the man beside her.

"Who owns this place?" she breathed out a frosty breath, but then she inhaled sharply as he placed his hand on top of hers where it rested on the black bars of the balcony.

"No one knows," he replied, following her gaze toward the torch-lined drive. "Some say it belongs to a reclusive man who only comes out during the autumn months." His mouth twitched at his own jest. "Others say it's haunted by a ghost, so no one dares to set foot inside."

"I sure hope it's haunted. That's rather exciting."

He laughed and turned toward her, leaning against the balcony with his elbows resting behind him. His lack of fear was admirable, and she dared to admit to herself that she enjoyed his carefree, ready-to-take-on-the-world attitude. It was…refreshing. Her home life didn't allow for such freedom and happiness.

His eyes sparkled with humor. "I also heard a ghost lives on the third floor. What do you say? Should we find out if it's friendly or malevolent?"

"You seem like you know your way around," she said, fluttering her eyelashes at him. "You lead."

Rather than returning through the trapdoor, the man's intense gaze held hers as he stepped closer and trapped her chin with gentle fingers.

Her entire body stilled with eager anticipation, a thrill shooting through her from her head to her toes. Already, this forbidden adventure was more than she ever dared to hope for. She hadn't known what to expect after stepping foot inside the estate. But it wasn't this.

And she loved every second of it.

She stood on her toes to meet him halfway until their lips met in the faintest brush like a whispered word of affection. Her stomach flipped and fluttered, her heart squeezing with joy and excitement.

More daringly, she smoothed her hands over his chest, his shoulders, and her fingers brushed playfully against the ties keeping his mask on his face. So desperately, she wanted to slip his mask off to reveal his identity. But she feared such knowledge might shatter the mysterious illusion the night offered.

The man groaned against her lips and pulled her closer, deepening the kiss, which she all too eagerly accepted. It was as if he felt the same spark. The same connection. The same happiness rising in her own chest.

He backed her up into the railing, and another thrill shot through her at the danger the kiss offered. If a single bar broke loose, they could plummet to their deaths.

And unfortunately, she loved the danger it posed.

A sigh escaped her as he trailed his kisses over her jaw, down her neck, and across her bare shoulders. His lips were fire. And she was the yearning kindling.

His attention returned to her mouth, his fingers threading through her hair, and his kisses slowing into something more gentle like a flickering candle flame rather than a blazing torch.

"I didn't attend the masquerade for this," he murmured, placing another kiss over a strand of her hair between his fingers. "To find someone. I was not expecting anything at all."

"Why *did* you come?"

"For escape."

"Same as I."

They held each other's gaze, and she realized they were more similar than she knew. Locked in a cage, banging at a sealed door with no way out. But tonight, they'd both found a way out. At least for a time. And she refused to squander what little time she might have remaining.

Running her finger over her lips, she smiled coyly. "You kissed me and we only just met."

"Like you said, tonight is a night for adventure and scandal."

Oh, she certainly liked him far more than she should, far more than what was appropriate, especially considering her status in society.

But she didn't care. Because she was just Vivi tonight.

"What is your name?" she asked. He opened his mouth as if to answer, but she quickly pressed a finger to his lips to stop his words. "Actually, don't tell me. It's more fun not knowing."

His lips pressed together with obvious discontent. "I don't want tonight to simply be a dream. To wake up in the morning to find out none of this was real. I don't want to let you go."

Warmth buried its seed in her heart, giving her hope. "Tonight won't end. I don't doubt you've come to the same conclusion as I have—we run in the same circle."

He nodded. "I have guessed as much."

She grinned, excitement radiating from her eyes. "Tonight won't end. Because when we find each other in the real world, our reunion will be that much sweeter."

Finally, the spark returned to his eyes, a smile to his handsome mouth as he grabbed her hand and led her to the trapdoor. "I believe we still have a ghost to hunt."

They laughed as they simultaneously attempted to sneak around the third floor hand in hand with discretion. But even over the loud music emanating from downstairs, she was sure others could hear them, the besotted fools they were.

A few rooms were locked or occupied, but for the most part, the party guests were downstairs or outside.

As they traveled down a darkened corridor, gooseflesh raised on her arms at the way the wind whistled through a crack in the windows, at the way door hinges groaned as if being opened slowly.

Vivienne tightened her grip on the man's hand as they slowed their pace before peering around the corner into an older, dustier part of the estate. Cobwebs hung from the ceiling. Furniture was scarred or broken. The wood floors were scratched. A chill lingered in the air, raising more gooseflesh on her arms and legs.

And then all too suddenly, a door slammed somewhere behind them.

Vivienne screamed, and the shriek that escaped the man spurred her heart into a fast, fearful rhythm. They continued to scream as they ran hand in hand down two flights of stairs, across velvety carpets leading to the back of the estate, and out the back entrance. They didn't stop running, even when rocks dug into her feet, even when the bite of cold air climbed up her neck and into her bones.

He threw open a random, empty carriage door. The two of them dove inside and slammed the door behind them. Only for silence to greet them.

Nothing chased them or tried to force their way into their small, protective space. All was quiet and normal and peaceful.

Finally, Vivienne realized just how silly they must have looked to passersby. She burst into laughter, sagging against the man where he was splayed out on the floor of the carriage. He soon joined in, and they were overcome with post-fear hysterics.

But then she quickly silenced his laughter by pulling him in for a heated kiss and then another until the bitter chill of autumn was dispelled by each passionate, heated breath. She didn't know how it was possible, how she could have already fallen for someone she'd only barely met. She wanted this to last. Not just for a single night. Not even for a week. But for many more months and years to come.

"What is the consensus?" he murmured against her lips.

"Oh, it most certainly is haunted," she replied as she loosened his cravat with desperate, eager fingers. "No doubt about it."

With a mischievous smile on her face and a wicked glint in her eye, she untied the curtains so they fell over the windows. And then shut the rest of the world out with a simple turn of a lock.

Chapter Two

"*Keep this safe for me,*" the beautiful masked woman had said as she'd cut a lock of her hair from her head and folded it within the safety of a handkerchief. And then she'd kissed him after tucking the handkerchief into his pocket. "*Until we find each other in the real world.*"

Edward Beaumont sighed as he carefully opened the soft white fabric to reveal a lock of her brown hair, perfectly preserved within her offering, a declaration of…something more.

It was all he dared to call it. The feeling felt like love. Like the first blossoms on a beautiful spring morning. But he knew better. Because the Edward who had fought off her ghosts and kissed her senseless? That man was strong and fearless, and he only existed rather infrequently, much to his dismay.

The reality of his life was much more…dismal.

Unable to part with the small piece of his mystery woman, he tucked the handkerchief into his pocket and attempted to sit up after nearly an entire week of being bedridden.

His head spun. His heart beat too fast. Dizziness all too quickly tried to claim him. He took several moments to breathe deeply to dispel the dizziness shrouding his mind and the weakness plaguing his body. The world finally stilled. But it was little comfort when all he wanted was to scour the entire city of Edilann to find the woman whose name he didn't even know.

The lock on the outside of his bedroom door jangled, keys clinking together on the opposite side, before the door opened, and his personal servant Cedric—or nanny as Edward liked to call him—barged inside with a bowl of hot broth resting on top of a silver platter. And beside the bowl…

Cedric's thick brown brows furrowed as he shook up the vial filled with yellow, translucent liquid and handed it to him. Edward didn't reach for it. He hated it. It did nothing to help the episodes.

"You must take your tonic," Cedric insisted. "It's for your own good."

"As is locking me up in this infuriating tower?"

The other man heaved a sigh as he sat at the foot of the bed, still holding out the tonic with a patient hand. "You snuck out *less* than a fortnight ago, and you are still recovering from its ill-effects. Of course, your sister would lock you in until you fully recover."

Edward smacked Cedric's hand. The vial flew out of his fingers and smashed into the ground in a puddle of glass and yellowish liquid. But his *nanny* only shook his head and produced another from inside his coat pocket.

"*I* am the lord of this house!" Edward bellowed, fighting through the dizziness in his head as he pushed himself to his feet. "I will not be caged in like some sort of…*animal!*"

But then his body swayed as he fought against the dizziness. Cedric patiently helped him sit back on the bed and squeezed his shoulders.

"Of course you are, Your Lordship." Cedric dipped his head in respect. "And your subjects need you to be well. Your sister is only trying to help."

Unable to help himself, he snorted as he finally resigned himself to throwing back the tonic, grimacing at the bitter flavor. "She's only trying to help herself. If she can keep me away from society, then I have no chance to marry. If I don't marry, I won't produce an heir. If I don't produce an heir, her son will take my place after I die."

Cedric frowned as he placed the bowl of broth at his bedside table. "You are able to go out plenty often enough."

"To see my friends," Edward pointed out dryly. "Who are all *male*."

"What is this really about?"

A despondent sigh escaped him as his gaze traveled toward the window, the first rays of morning filtering through the warped glass. Even the glass caged him in, keeping him from the real world when he so desperately wanted to be a part of it.

"I met a woman. And I can't stay in here, wasting away when I need to find her." He quirked his mouth to the side as he returned his attention to Cedric. "I apologize for smacking you. I am frustrated with Clara. You are not to blame."

"I know how much you dislike the tonic. But the physician said it should help."

"Yet, it doesn't."

"It just needs time."

"It's been years, Cedric. If it hasn't gotten better by now, it never will."

The man didn't refute him.

"Where is Clara this morning?" he asked, allowing Cedric to help get him dressed. He most often did the task himself, but some days it proved difficult.

"Calling on a few friends, Your Lordship."

He nodded, hatching a plan in his head. Clara didn't leave the estate often enough. Today was his only chance at escape. "I'd like to go on a walk." When his servant started to protest, Edward quickly cut in. "Just a short walk. I think getting fresh air might do me good over being cooped up in this tower."

Despite his dizziness and heavy chest, he climbed down the stairs of his tower with Cedric following only a few steps behind. When they exited the estate, he inhaled a deep breath of fresh air, taking in his surroundings.

Pine trees lined most of the property, giving it an isolated, woodsy feel. A dirt path led to a private lake where he liked to enjoy the quiet solitude of fishing—or rather, Cedric's quiet companionship. Another dirt path led around the property large enough for a carriage to traverse for a leisurely drive.

Although the main city of Edilann was close, he felt snug in his little nook near the mountainside.

The transition of warm air to cold brushed along his face, signaling the turn of the next season. Autumn splashed a variety of colors from red to yellow to orange across the beautiful mountain canvas before him.

This place...

It brought him peace in an otherwise confusing world filled with loneliness and heartache. But perhaps he wouldn't be so lonely if…if he could find *her*.

With Cedric at his side, they traversed a small dirt path leading to the stables, and a wave of relief washed over him when the scents of horse and hay greeted him as he entered. His horse, Walnut, snorted upon seeing him, prancing back and forth in her stall as he approached with an apple in his hand. In only two bites, the mare gobbled it up and stuck her face through a gap in the wood, sniffing him in search of more food.

"I'll give you more later," he promised as he stroked the gentle creature's velvety nose.

He glanced over his shoulder to find Cedric tending to his own horse—a gift given to him as per the agreement of his work contract with the family. And thankfully, the horse occupied his attention long enough for Edmund to quietly ask the stable boy to saddle his horse, as he hadn't the strength to do so on his own today.

But the moment Cedric glanced in his direction, he frowned, following him out of the stable as he led Walnut by the reins.

"Where are you going?" the other man asked, following close at his heels as Edward led the mare away from the barn.

"I have to go find her, Cedric."

"You cannot leave the estate. Don't you remember what happened when you journeyed to Avorstead?"

He frowned as he recalled the time months ago when he and his friends took the week-long trip to Avorstead in the kingdom of Leonia and back to locate another mutual friend named Barnaby. The man had lost his memories and had been staying with a family of sisters, at least until they'd retrieved him and brought him back home. Barnaby had ended up marrying one of those women and was now living happily in Edilann, his memories intact, with his wife, Ivette.

"I was with my friends. I was fine."

"*Was*," Cedric emphasized, now falling into step beside him. "You were bedridden for two weeks after the fact."

He released a disgruntled huff and turned his shoulder toward the man. Unfortunately, Cedric wasn't done speaking.

"And where do you suppose you'll start looking? Hmm?" He ticked off on his fingers. "You don't even know her name. Where she lives. Who her family is. The places she frequents." The man sighed when Edward continued forward as if he hadn't spoken at all. "At least take a carriage."

"My sister would never allow it."

Oh, he loved his sister. But after the death of their parents on a voyage across the sea years ago, she was far too protective for her own good.

Placing his foot into the stirrup, he swung his leg up and over the saddle. The quick movement caused his head to spin, and he focused on taking deep breaths until his surroundings stilled once more.

"Just...*wait*." Cedric sighed again and gestured toward the stables. "I'll escort you into town."

Edward scoffed. "I'm not so fragile as that."

In fact, the thought irked him that his sister forced someone to remain in his company at all times.

Without waiting for the other man to mount up, Edward turned his horse toward the dirt path leading over the ground of the estate and kicked the creature's flanks.

The horse started into a trot, and then its gait smoothed into a gallop. Wind tore at his black hair, the strands flitting over his forehead and eyes. He brushed it out of his face before holding on tighter to the reins.

The crisp yellow and orange terrain flew past in a whir of motion. Fallen leaves crunched beneath the horse's hooves. The scent of death and decay wafted past his nose, making drawing air difficult.

His head spun. His heart squeezed and jumped, flipped and flopped. He felt his pulse ricocheting within his veins, spurting faster and faster until it stole the breath from him entirely.

No! he internally shouted at himself. *I am strong enough to do this simple task.*

But even as he slowed his mount to a trot to try to regain some of his breath, his head felt light and dizzy. His heart squeezed painfully, stealing the remaining air from his lungs. He tried to dismount when black dots shrouded his vision. But his lightheadedness won. And rather than dismounting smoothly from a moving horse, he ungracefully lost control of his limbs, tipped precariously to the side, and landed with a painful heap on a bed of grass and dirt.

He gasped for air, but the breath struggled through his lungs, making the fight for consciousness difficult when his lungs spasmed and his heart raced.

"Edward!" Cedric's voice floated far away. "Edward!"

He clawed at the grass, trying to get himself into a sitting position. He nearly gave up when a pair of strong arms lifted him enough to help him sit, and they kept him upright even as each shallow breath struggled in and out of his body.

"Stay with me," Cedric ordered in a terse tone. "Slow breaths. There you go. That's it."

Although his breathing still came quickly, his heart calmed, and the shadows in his eyes slowly dissipated until finally, he gained enough control of his lungs to take unhurried breaths.

Edward exhaled a long sigh and slumped exhaustedly against his servant. "I'm sorry," he murmured. It was all he had strength enough to say.

"Your sister will want to know—"

"Tell her and you're fired." The threat sounded weak at best, especially when no force lay behind it.

"You have no jurisdiction over whether I keep my job, Eddie. I have your best interests at heart." The man patted his shoulder. "The doctor will want to see you again."

"No." He struggled to sit by himself when his body was plagued by weakness. "I need to find her."

"And you shall. Just not like this."

With an aching chest and bleary eyes, he gazed toward the path leading into the city. If he hadn't found her by now…he feared it might somehow be too late.

Chapter Three

How much more *seen* could Vivienne make herself? She huffed in frustration as she twirled the umbrella she held in wrist-length white gloves, carefully watching passersby in the royal gardens as she conversed with several other ladies of the court. Four weeks had passed since she'd said goodbye to her mysterious masked man, and ever since, she'd gone out of her way to attend every social event possible. Including dreary tea-time activities all around the kingdom.

Unfortunately, Sir Mask was elusive, a difficult man to catch. She'd practically scoured the entire kingdom for him, under the guise of being socially enthusiastic, of course.

Yet, it was as if he'd disappeared entirely. She would have run into him if he were looking for her, too.

If, she emphasized in her mind.

A part of her feared the sparks that had flown between them was only one sided. But she refused to give up hope. That night, she'd wanted more than just one evening with him, and the feeling had only grown stronger in their time apart.

Several men only a few years older than her passed by, dipping their heads in acknowledgement. Vivienne tipped her umbrella down to cover the top half of their faces while watching their mouths move in greeting.

A despondent sigh escaped her when she recognized none belonging to Sir Mask.

Queasiness rolled through her stomach at the thought of not finding him at all. This was supposed to be a fun game. But she hadn't expected the game to stretch more than a week or two. She should have asked him his name. She regretted not doing so.

What if he left Edilann? she silently asked herself. *What if he's gone?*

Bile climbed her throat, and she took several deep breaths to calm herself. Unfortunately, the queasiness refused to abate as regret became her constant shadow.

A chilly autumn breeze picked up around her skirts, the bite of the air and the white of the skies promising a storm. Big, fat snowflakes drifted down from the heavens, twirling and leaping and flurrying around her in a dance of white powder.

She'd always loved the snow. It was cold and mysterious and filled with unspoken adventure. But now? It caused panic to race through her. Soon enough, she wouldn't be able to venture outside at all. If she didn't find the masked man before the snow started to stick, she might never find him at all.

"Shall we head back inside?" one of the other ladies suggested. Despite the threat of cold the snow offered, the other woman's gaze trailed the men as they traveled down the path.

Vivienne waved the others away. "I will be but a moment. I simply would like to admire the snow for a while longer."

The others left her in the garden, giggling as they fell into step with the men.

She lifted her gaze to the flurries of snow, watching how they danced and twirled like performers on a stage. The movement was soft and beautiful and also filled with immense loneliness in the accompanying silence.

All too quickly, her stomach churned with intense sickness. She turned, and unable to help herself, she vomited into the bare rosebush to her right.

Her eyes snapped wide open when realization dawned on her. The thought of never seeing the mysterious man again plagued her with dread, but not with sickness.

This was…

…something else.

Her hand flew to her belly as shock overcame her. As denial wedged itself into her mind and clung on with fierce talons. All she managed was to stare blankly at the path ahead as the silence pressed down heavily on her shoulders until it managed to crush her.

Because…her monthly bleeding was late. By two weeks.

"No, no, no!" she cried, frantically glancing around to make sure no one had seen her purge her insides into a rosebush. But only bare trees and shrubs stared back at her where they circled a sundial. She was alone.

What was she to do? This wasn't supposed to happen. She wasn't married yet. This couldn't happen to her. Her father would kill her, and as the warlord of Edilann, she feared he would quite literally kill the man responsible.

Taking a deep breath and letting it out slowly, she pressed a hand to her breast and closed her eyes to reach for her inner calm. Surely, this was a hoax. Just a scare. Sometimes her bleedings would arrive late for no reason other than whim. This was nothing. It would pass.

But as one week turned into two, she could no longer deny it.

She was with child.

It became increasingly difficult to keep down her meals and hide her ailing condition from her friends and family members. But most of all, it was difficult to hide it from the servants. She'd pricked her finger to coat her undergarments with blood. She'd spent nearly a week bedridden with "womanly aches," but in reality, all her body wanted to do was vomit.

All efforts to find her masked man ceased when fear plagued her day after day. She couldn't hide her condition for long. She knew that. Especially when she eventually started showing. But she was scared. Terrified. And perhaps there was only one person she could turn to.

She took a deep breath as she stood outside the closed doors of one of the drawing rooms in the palace. Muffled voices and laughter came from within, inspiring more anxiety to wriggle into her bloodstream and spur her heart into a fast rhythm.

She shifted her weight from foot to foot on the soft blue carpet, reaching deep within herself for the courage she needed to face this.

Finally, she turned the handle and stepped inside. All conversation ceased. All eyes turned to her.

Through the bile trying to climb her throat, she managed a smile as her gaze found her mother where she sat on an ornate settee. "What a beautiful gathering," she said, curtsying to her aunt, the queen herself, and to several other ladies of the court. "Mother, might I steal you for a few moments? One of the family birds got out, and I can't find it anywhere."

It was code for needing her immediate help, and it couldn't wait.

Mother smiled to the others as she set down her cup of tea. "I will try to make it back in a timely manner. I've so enjoyed all of your company."

The woman made a graceful exit, and they fell into step beside one another before entering a vacant room filled with ornate, velvety furniture. Light spilled between blue velvet drapes over the windows, the color representing the kingdom of Edilann.

The moment the door closed behind them, her mother's forehead creased with worry, and she smoothed down her coiffed brown hair like she always did when in distress. "What is it, dear? What happened?"

Unable to help herself when her emotions now had a mind of their own, she burst into tears. They came faster than she could wipe them away. "I made a mistake," she sobbed, staring at the floor so she didn't have to look her mother in the eye.

"We all make mistakes, dear," her mother said calmly as she stroked Vivienne's hair.

"You don't understand." She finally braved lifting her head and decided to speak the truth quickly to get it over with. "I am with child."

Her mother's mouth closed, her jaw clenching as she took a step backward. Her gaze jumped toward the door, and without preamble, she grabbed Vivienne's arm and dragged her closer to the windows as if to prevent them from being overheard.

"You are sure?" she asked.

Vivienne nodded. "I'm quite certain."

A long breath whooshed from her mother's lips as she pinched the bridge of her nose. "Who is the father?"

"I don't know!"

"Vivienne!" her mother gasped.

"No, I mean I *know* who it is. I just don't know his name. I don't know where to find him."

Slowly, her mother lowered herself onto a velvety chair and smoothed her skirts, regaining her earlier poise. "Listen carefully, Vivi."

Vivienne followed suit and sat in another chair, dread and terror tangling in her stomach.

Continuing, her mother said, "No one, and I repeat *no one*, is to hear of what you just told me. Not even the father of this child."

"But—"

Her mother stopped her words with a hard grip on her arm. "I am here to help you, Vivi. If *anyone* learns of this, you will doom every single one of your siblings to a life of being shunned by their peers. No one will marry your sisters. We will be cast out of polite society."

She wiped several more tears from her face. How could she have been so selfish? How could she have let this happen? "What must I do?"

"The only thing you can do." Her mother sat up straighter and looked her dead in the eye. "You must marry. And quickly now."

Emotion clogged her throat. Her eyelids shuttered closed. She was eighteen years old. Of course, she knew plenty of people who were married by that age. But she'd wanted excitement and adventure and to have a little bit of fun before marriage clipped her wings.

But it seemed she'd had one bit of fun too many.

"I have feelings for this man," she said in a husky whisper, opening her eyes to gaze back at her mother through blurry tears. "I don't want to marry another."

"Tell me more about him."

So, she explained everything. Where she'd met him. Why she was so taken with him. His endearing qualities. His physical attributes. That he ran in the same circle as her.

Mother nodded slowly, taking in all the information. "He sounds like a decent man of good breeding." But then she rolled her eyes. "I said *decent*. He should not have taken liberties with you." She sighed, disappointment in her very breath. "We will try to find this man. But if we don't… I will arrange a marriage for you. Like I said, we don't have much time before you start showing. This must be quick."

Vivienne understood the reasoning behind a quick marriage. But a physical ache still pounded on her chest. Hopelessness sat heavy on her shoulders. How long had she spent trying to find the masked man? It was more likely she would wed another than locate him in a timely manner.

"And what of Father?"

Shifting in her seat, Mother scoffed and smoothed down her skirts once again. "I love your father, but he will sooner blow this out of proportion than protect the family with silence. He will *never* find out. Otherwise, this entire family will be ruined. This is only between you and me."

After letting out a long breath, Vivienne placed a hand over her churning belly, hardly believing something was growing inside of her. "And the baby's father?"

Her mother's expression became grave. "It is best he doesn't know either until after you've secured yourself in the marriage. We don't want to give him any reason to back out of the commitment."

Another wave of dread crashed over her. She steepled her fingers together over her face and closed her eyes. She wanted to disappear, to pretend like she hadn't fouled up so badly as to have to face the consequences of her actions.

"What now?" she asked in a barely audible whisper.

"I have several invitations from those within our circle. We will attend every single one of them under the guise of your interest in securing yourself a husband. But Vivi…I will only give you two weeks to find this man, and the wedding will go through only if I approve of him. Understand?"

Wordlessly, she nodded, her eyes still closed. As much as she regretted clipping her own wings…

She would do what she must for the sake of her family.

Chapter Four

One thing Edward was excellent at was performing his duties as viscount. Much of the time, the work didn't require him getting out of a chair, which allowed him to rest and gain back his strength. The more he rested, the easier it was to perform more strenuous tasks.

And the more he rested…the easier it would be to search Edilann for the masked woman. After how terrible the last incident was, he couldn't risk another outing until he recovered from the weakness plaguing his body and the dizziness in his mind. Sometimes recovery took days. Other times weeks.

A long sigh escaped him as he pushed his work aside in favor of pulling out the brown lock of hair from his vest pocket. He reverently stroked the hair with a finger, an ache of sadness welling within his heart.

What if he ended up finding her? Could she accept him? Condition and all? What if his search only broke his heart more? Was it worth the risk?

Before he managed to answer his own question, Clara strutted by in a whoosh of silky blue skirts. She wore a hat over her coiffed black hair and a white fur wrap over her shoulders. Like always, she didn't spare a glance for him when she was often in such a hurry to exit the house without him inquiring of her.

But he inquired, anyway.

"Where are you headed?"

Clara waved away his question with a flick of her hand. "Nowhere important."

He pushed himself out of his chair and followed, his shoes slapping against the marble floors in his haste. "Where?"

"Just a small dinner party. Nothing extravagant."

"I'm coming, too."

But just as he reached for a coat hanging near the door, she turned to him with a pitying look in blue eyes similar to his own. "I already responded to the invitation, reserving only one seat. I thought you were too sick to attend, you see. Perhaps next time might be a better opportunity."

Without another word, Clara exited the estate and slammed the door resoundingly behind her.

For a long few moments, Edward stared at the door closed between him and the freedom of the outside world. Seven entire miserable weeks had passed since the masquerade. *Seven!* And he was no closer to finding his mystery woman.

Anger coursed through his veins as he pushed the drapes aside to watch as his sister's carriage disappeared into the night, smooth and quick as if she had planned to slight him all along. What must other members of his circle think of him?

"Cedric," Edward said in a quiet, dangerous tone. His servant glanced up from his book in the corner of the room.

If he couldn't go to events due to his sister's gatekeeping, then he would bring everyone to him. "Ready a carriage. We're going to see a friend."

"I am entirely offended you thought I would be home on a night such as this!" Lord Barnaby Mavis scoffed as he poured himself a glass of water and downed it in a single gulp.

Edward raised an eyebrow, glancing down at his friend's attire. He wore a loose shirt over breeches, a robe tied around his clothing as if he'd only recently woken from a nap.

"You're a newly wedded man." He shrugged and took the water glass Barnaby offered him. "Don't all of you usually hunker down with your wives for the first year? *Of course*, I thought you'd be home rather than peacocking about the streets."

Barnaby scoffed again as he lifted a finger from his glass to point at him. "Just you wait. Your turn will arrive soon enough."

Melancholy sank to the bottom of his stomach at the thought. Edilann law stated that nobility needed to be married by the age of twenty-four, and he would turn twenty-four at the end of the year. Honestly, his bachelordom wasn't for lack of trying. Courting was simply…difficult for him.

He turned his attention away to take in the lavish room. Thick, velvety drapes. A fire crackling in the hearth. Refreshments covering one of the tables on the opposite side of the room.

He picked up a honey cake from a silver platter and stood in front of the warm fire. "I need your help."

"Oh?" Barnaby raised an eyebrow, the sleep suddenly gone and replaced by intrigue. "What can I do for you that you can't accomplish yourself?"

What his friend really meant was that they were both titled, Barnaby an earl and him a viscount. They were wealthy with plenty of connections. But his friend didn't truly understand his dire circumstances because he tried his best to hide his condition. He'd lost so many people already. He refused to lose his friends, too.

"I need help finding someone. My sister has…made things difficult."

His friend snorted. "Doesn't approve of the lady, does she? And don't try to protest. This has *lady friend* written all over it."

"Well…actually, I don't know her name. She has brown hair. Dark brown eyes. A bit of a sultry look around her lips."

With a quirk of his mouth, Barnaby set his glass down and crossed his ankle over his knee before brushing the blond sweep of his hair out of his eyes. "You described at least twelve dozen women of my acquaintance."

"But…she's heart-stoppingly beautiful. A few freckles over her face. She's a bit mischievous and headstrong. Probably doesn't quite fit the mold of women in our society."

Barnaby scratched his chin. Rather than mocking him for his fixation on this woman, he genuinely seemed like he wanted to help. "You narrowed down the choices, most definitely. It's a start." He clapped his hands on his knees. "Let's do for you what my mother did for me. She hosted a ball to draw Ivette out before we were reunited. We shall do the same for you."

Oh, so many things were wrong with the idea. Could he risk it?

But as he recalled the mystery woman's confidence and rebellious demeanor, he realized he must be brave. Just one little act of rebellion of his own.

"Clara would never allow it."

His friend laughed and shook his head. "You are a viscount, Edward. You can do as you please. But..." He leaned forward and leveled him with a stare. "If we send out the invitations behind her back, she either has to publicly apologize for canceling the event, which would cause scandal and great embarrassment, or go out of her way to make it happen. I don't doubt she'll do the latter."

"You are devious."

"I am, aren't I?" Barnaby's eyes twinkled with amusement. "She'll never find out until it's too late."

A seed of hope planted in his heart. "I need to borrow stationery. A lot of it."

The barn door crashed open, startling the animals inside into a frenzy. Edward's heart gave an enormous start as he reeled backward off the stool he stood on, barely catching himself on the smooth wooden door leading to his horse's stall.

But then his stomach twisted with dread when he faced the fury in Clara's face, her body a silhouette against the backdrop of the early morning sunshine behind her.

"Everyone *out!*" she shouted.

Cedric and the stable boy scrambled for the exit in a shuffle of desperate feet. Edward gauged the distance between his sister and the safety of escape. Finding no way out of the entrapment, he backed up until his shoulders brushed against the stall. Walnut nibbled on his clothing as if trying to offer comfort and encouragement.

"You did this behind my back?" She waved an invitation wildly in the air with a white-gloved hand, and as she stepped farther into the stables, he realized she wore nice clothing as if she'd gone out to see a friend. "Everyone knew about it before I did. You made me a fool!"

His sister moved too quickly to dodge. Her hand struck him across the cheek. Pain flared in his face. He lowered his gaze to the ground. When he found it difficult to form a coherent reply, she struck him again and again before shoving his shoulders and causing his head to hit the stall behind him.

The horse whinnied with agitation, pacing back and forth, back and forth.

Injustice and self-preservation reared within him, but he remained still and unmoving. Gentlemen did not hit back. He would not lower himself to what he suspected Clara's husband had done to her before leaving his family behind.

"You are *nothing!*" Clara hissed. "You won't live much longer. The doctor has confirmed it. So, step back and let me handle estate matters. It will be my responsibility when you are gone, anyway."

Clara straightened her clothing and glared as she gestured to his raw cheek. "This is your fault. If you would stop sneaking out and doing things behind my back, I wouldn't have to punish you."

And then she spun on her heel, exiting the stables in a flurry of skirts, leaving silence in her wake.

A numbness crawled up Edward's legs and into his chest as he forced himself to feel nothing. Not sadness or regret. Just…nothing.

He slipped into Walnut's stall and began brushing the brown mare down, his movement remaining steady even as he heard hesitant footsteps approaching.

"Eddie?" Cedric asked in a quiet, worried tone.

Edward shifted his body so the horse's neck hid his face, blazing on one side. This wasn't the first time Clara had struck him, and Cedric knew it. But what could a servant do to intervene in family affairs? At best, he would be fired. And despite how Edward threatened to sack him on occasion, he couldn't bear the thought of him leaving. Because what would he have left if his only friend at the estate was gone?

"Wait outside," he finally managed in a raspy tone. "Please."

After a few more seconds of hesitation, Cedric did as he asked, leaving him alone in the stables.

At least, he thought he was alone before he caught faint sniffling in another stall. His eyebrows drew together, and slowly, he exited his stall and approached another, opening the door to find his nephew, James, huddled in the corner, tears trailing from amber-colored eyes, pieces of hay sticking out of his black hair.

Even at five years old, too much responsibility was placed on his shoulders. Edward remembered the feeling all too well. When he'd been a child, so much had depended on him and his health as the next in line for the title.

"Why are you upset?" Edward asked quietly as he joined the boy on a bale of hay as he continued to wipe his eyes.

"I hate it when Mama yells at you and hits you. She's so mean."

Edward said nothing, even though he agreed with the child. His sister was five years his senior, and she had only grown nastier and bolder after her husband had left the kingdom and abandoned his family years ago.

"She cares about you."

The poor boy shook his head. "She doesn't. She sometimes yells at me, too."

Because she's hurting.

But that gave her no right to treat them this way.

He pressed his lips together and hung his head. His eyes stung as he wrapped an arm around James' shoulders and drew him into a side embrace. "I care about you."

James sniffed into Edward's shoulder. "I want a papa. I wish you could be my papa."

He blinked rapidly when he was all too close to losing control of his emotions. "Uncles can be there for you, too. I'll never leave you."

"Promise?"

His troubled gaze shifted to his lap as he recalled what his sister had said. Did the doctor truly think he wouldn't live much longer?

Still, he squeezed his nephew endearingly and said, "I promise."

Chapter Five

A despondent sigh escaped Vivienne as she stepped down from the carriage, returning home after another fruitless outing. She was starting to think this mysterious, masked man didn't exist. The two allotted weeks were almost up, and she still had nothing to show for it.

She tightened her fur shawl around her shoulders, watching as a foggy breath left her lips after another sigh. These outings were taxing on her exhausted body. Every waking moment, rather than resting like she ought to, she had to hide her condition by being seen and by attending event after event until she wanted to drop. It didn't help that the longer she remained upright, the more she wanted to vomit.

Holding it in was one of the hardest things she'd had to do.

Following her mother inside the palace, she allowed a servant to take her wrap and followed her mother to their family's suite in the west wing of the castle. As she climbed the long length of the curved staircase, she absently trailed her fingers over the smooth wood of the railing, her feet treading plush carpet.

Servants passed with a slight bow or curtsy. She hardly had the strength to acknowledge them when she simply wanted to collapse and fall asleep for several weeks.

Finally, when they reached the suites, everyone absent except the two of them and their twittering yellow canaries in cages, Vivienne loosened the strings on her corset and sighed in relief as she slumped onto the settee with her feet up. Her clothing was starting to get tighter. Soon enough, she would have to wear a different style of clothing altogether.

Thank the Mother Goddess it's almost winter.

She would be able to hide her condition for a while longer wearing a shawl.

Mother tapped her fan in her palm as she surveyed Vivienne up and down. "We cannot wait any longer. You will marry Duke Hastings."

"You promised me a few more days."

"I've changed my mind. We are standing on perilous ground."

Vivienne didn't protest as she covered her face with her elbow. Hot, silent tears trailed down her cheeks as she recalled deep blue eyes, a breathtaking smile, and a spirit that matched hers in energy and playfulness. She would be losing so much.

But what more could she do? She had done everything that could possibly be done.

The tears quickly fell over her cheeks and seeped into her hair. Tears of heartache. Of frustration. Of hopelessness. What a dreary life she would have married to the monotone, self-enamored duke. The thought disgusted her. It dampened her spirits. Of course, she knew other women near her age who had married men twice older than them. Sometimes it was just the way things were. And perhaps it wouldn't have been so bad if she hadn't already fallen for another.

"Oh!" her mother gasped, making her jump.

"What is it?" She bolted upright and dried her tears, quickly joining her mother's side. The older woman held an invitation to a party hosted by Lord Beaumont.

She perked up at the name. Years ago, they had been the best of friends. What had happened in the seven years of their separation? Although she hadn't seen him in a long time, she'd seen the man's sister at least a hundred times.

She released a long breath, trying her best to keep her meal down when the jarring movement of leaping to her feet churned her stomach in the most horrid way.

Mother tapped the invitation with a finger. "Lord Beaumont matches the physical description you gave me. I can't believe I hadn't thought of him before now. He's so...*elusive*. Doesn't attend gatherings very often."

Vivienne snatched the invitation from her mother, scanning the words several times before they finally sank in. The party was scheduled a few days from now, a formal event. "You think this could be him?"

"If it isn't, then I have no choice but to marry you to the duke."

She made a face. The duke was overly vain and selfish to the point of annoyance. He stood too close and his breath sometimes smelled of rot. Oh, and he was twice her age.

Nodding distractedly, her mother took the invitation back and wandered across the room. "Wear your red gown for this event. It looks best with your hair color and skin tone. Plus, it's a bit more…snug in the upper bodice."

"Mother!"

The other woman smiled apologetically. "You have a possible viscount to catch. You must use every asset available to you."

Stress and anxiety ate away at her as she wrung one of her gloves between her fingers, pacing back and forth across the room. "It's been seven weeks. If it *is* him, and he's been so close all this time… Perhaps he never wanted to find me in the first place."

Her mother took her by the shoulders and squeezed. "We are *Winfields*! We take what we want and forge our own path. You will have that man eating out of the palm of your hand before you're done with him."

Her eyes smarted at her mother's kind words, and she threw her arms around her shoulders. "What would I do without you?"

"I am your mother. We are on the same side, darling. And we will see this succeed."

She hoped so with all her heart. She couldn't bear the thought of being the reason shadows were cast upon her family. She would fix this. Somehow, everything would work out fine.

Over the course of days, Edward avoided Clara. But truly, he needn't even bother, as she was far too busy taking over the preparations for the party that it took every ounce of her attention. And when the day finally arrived, he couldn't help but feel smug satisfaction when society expected him to play the attentive host as lord of the house, and Clara had no excuse to lock him away in his room.

A shaky exhale escaped him when his head felt too light, and his heart misbehaved. But this time, he wasn't sure if it was due to his condition or from nerves.

Was the masked woman going to show up?

If so, who was she? Would he recognize her?

He stood at the opposite end of the ballroom, watching as guests entered with excitement written on their faces. They reveled at the wintry decorations of pine and red berries, at the music drifting elegantly through the large room, at the mountains of refreshments servants offered on silver platters. He tried to look past the sea of green, blue, and purple skirts, past the gentlemen escorting their ladies inside, and studied each face.

His gaze quickly flitted over blonde hair and remained longer on the brunettes. After greeting dozens of guests, his hopes deflated when he didn't recognize any of them as his mystery woman.

A servant passed by with a glass of wine. He reached for the stem of the glass and threw it back quickly before Cedric managed to snatch it away.

The man in question held out a hand as if he'd been in the process of reaching for it, but then his lips pressed together, and he took several steps back, his gaze staring ahead.

Alcohol made his condition worse. But tonight, he needed it. Otherwise, he wasn't sure how to survive his nerves.

"There you are!" Uncle Maxwell's voice boomed excitedly across the room as he approached with outstretched arms, pulling him in for a brief embrace. "You have a talent for blending in with the wall."

Edward chuckled, his nerves dissolving the slightest bit with the comfort of his uncle's presence. The man had been like a second father since his own had passed years ago. "I wasn't sure you would make it. I thought you were on a trip across the sea."

He clapped him on the shoulder and downed a drink himself. "I returned two days ago. Wouldn't want to miss my nephew's party. They happen only once in an eon." His attention perked up as if he spotted someone across the room. "I'll find you later. I have to catch up with a few friends."

His uncle squeezed his shoulder before weaving through the crowd in the opposite direction.

The scent of sweet pastries wafted past Edward's nose, and he snatched one from a platter as well, nibbling on it to give him something to do other than fret. If he didn't find the woman *tonight*, he likely would have no chance at all.

"You look strung tight," a voice said behind him, and he spun around to find a familiar head of blond hair and blue eyes staring back at him.

"Thank the stars you're here," he groaned. "I thought I'd have to face this alone."

"This as in meeting your mystery woman?" Barnaby chuckled, his eyes scanning the growing crowd. "Is she here?"

Edward shrugged. "I don't know." But then he scratched his arm anxiously. "I would recognize her if she was, wouldn't I? Or do you think I've already forgotten what she looks like?"

"I highly doubt you've forgotten. But it certainly makes things difficult if you've only really seen the bottom half of her face."

He groaned again, running his fingers through his hair, when he thought of something else to churn his stomach into a tangled mess. What if *she* had forgotten him? Weeks had passed. And although she'd been on his mind every single day, he worried the memory of him had slipped her mind entirely.

"I think I might be sick."

Barnaby slapped him on the shoulder. "Hold it together for a little longer. People are still arriving."

Taking a long, deep breath, he stood straighter and greeted more guests. It was only a matter of time before she showed up. Surely.

Vivienne smoothed her hair for the dozenth time. She fixed her bodice, struggling to breathe when everything felt far too tight. She pinched her cheeks when her churning stomach had stolen all traces of color from her face and left her with a pale complexion.

Her mind was in a daze as she exited the carriage in the darkness of night and stared back at a beautiful estate surrounded by dazzling pines, flickering torchlight, and a warm, welcoming feel to the exterior of the large home.

Taking a deep breath, she smoothed down her dress as she allowed a servant to take her cloak, and then she stepped inside.

A whoosh of warm air washed over her, followed by the feeling of…safety. Of relief. She didn't know what else to call the sensation other than returning home. Almost as if she'd been here before.

Almost as if...

She inhaled sharply, recalling a time long ago of running through these halls. Climbing trees. Riding horses. Laughing beneath the stars. And most of all, she remembered a pair of dark blue eyes crinkled with happiness and warmth.

In the years that had passed, she'd almost forgotten. But now...

"We've been here before," she gasped quietly to her mother as they walked down a lavish hallway decorated with pine garlands.

Mother smiled softly, but a deep sadness lived within her eyes. "Lady Beaumont was my dearest friend. She and her husband went on a voyage to find a cure for...well, I can't remember what. But they never returned home, declared dead long ago. Edward Beaumont had still been only a boy at their passing. His sister took over the estate for a time until he came of age."

The memories flashed through her mind faster now. Long hours with the horses. An afternoon fishing beside the lake. Most of the memories she had with Edward were filled with joy and laughter in the outdoors. If she recalled correctly, he was four or five years older than her.

But then her stomach dipped when she remembered him spending days, weeks in bed with a terrible illness. She didn't know what the illness had been, only that he had recovered later.

She had not seen her childhood friend in a long time. Could he possibly be the masked man she'd met at the masquerade?

She quickened her steps, needing to know the truth.

She burst inside the ballroom, hardly sparing a thought or word for anyone else when her gaze darted frantically about.

Edward, Edward, Edward.

Her heart beat his name through her veins in her desperate attempt to locate him. Mother followed close at her heels, apologizing to others about her behavior, claiming she was simply excited about the event.

But then her heart seemed to cease beating altogether as her gaze landed on a man with black hair longer in the front than in the back.

Vivienne's mouth dried, and her heart beat unbearably fast, her hands perspiring with nervous anxiety. With a single glance, she knew it was him. The man from the masquerade. The slight curve of his lips was unmistakable. The dark blue of his eyes had been imprinted on her heart. And she recalled the sweep of his black hair tangled in her fingers, his sweet mouth showering her in kisses.

"I found him," she said breathlessly as if her lungs couldn't draw air in his presence. He stood in a circle of three other men and two women. She recognized Lord Barnaby Mavis and Sir Tobie Lambton. She'd seen Sir Charles Lockwood around the palace.

As for the identity of her masked man, she only dared to hope…

Her mother followed her gaze before her eyes sparkled with excitement. "The black-haired one? Yes! That's Edward Beaumont. The viscount. The man I was talking about. You're positive it's him?"

Vivienne placed a hand to her fluttering belly as her gaze roamed over him. She recognized his broad shoulders and tall stature. The way he flipped his hair out of his eyes. The way his mouth curved when someone must have voiced a jest. "I'm almost certain." But...there was something different about him. A tentative expression lingered on his face, and his stance didn't exude confidence like the man she'd met at the masquerade.

"Then let us go to him. You've charmed him once." Her mother scoffed as she opened her fan and leisurely made her way toward the viscount. "Surely, you can do it again."

Yet, she had an audience of six, plus her mother. Charming him with people looking on would not be easy.

Fear crept up within her as they moved nearer to the group. He'd had *weeks* to find her! And heaven knew she'd been searching far too long to find him. What if he'd forgotten about her? What if he didn't care anymore?

Her heart pounding against her ribcage, she withdrew her fan from her reticule and popped it open. And just as they stood before the group, she "accidentally" dropped her fan at his feet.

"Oh," he murmured, stooping down to pick it up. He was still crouched when he lifted his head, and their gazes locked.

Edward's mouth fell open, and he simply stared back at her, at a loss for words. Now that he was closer, she knew without a doubt he was the man from the masquerade. The same dark blue eyes. The same tone of voice. And he gazed at her as if dumbstruck, his open mouth familiar in the most pleasant ways.

She took a small measure of satisfaction that he seemed to recognize her, too.

"Lord Beaumont, what a pleasure to be invited to this splendid event," her mother said, breaking them out of their daze long enough for him to stand and pull his gaze from her and fix his attention on her mother. He immediately bowed at the waist, recognizing her superior rank. "I don't suppose you remember my daughter, Lady Vivienne Winfield. The two of you used to spend hours and hours playing together as children."

Edward silently mouthed an obvious profanity as he glanced back toward her, his face pale with something akin to terror. He likely feared her father and what the warlord might do to him should he find out about their passionate rendezvous.

Vivienne curtsied and gave him a demure smile. "I am honored to be reacquainted with you, Your Lordship." Her eyes sparkled with mischief, her meaning coming across a different way between the two of them.

Behind him, Lord Mavis elbowed Edward in the back. He coughed and held out a hand to her. "The pleasure is mine," he squeaked, and she found it difficult to stifle a laugh. She only barely managed to restrain herself.

She placed her hand in his, her stomach flipping pleasantly as he lifted her hand and bestowed a light kiss over her fingers.

But all too quickly, he dropped her hand and glanced over her shoulder. She knew he was looking for her father. He wasn't attending the event tonight, thank the stars.

"Perhaps, Lord Beaumont," she said in an attempt to bring his attention back to her, "you might seek me out later for a dance."

He shook his head. "I am not dancing tonight. I will owe you for the next event."

Unease pinched her in the gut as she searched his eyes for…for what, exactly? He was cold and aloof and seemingly uninterested. Where was the confident, flirtatious, playful man she'd met weeks ago?

Because he was not here.

Without a word, Vivienne curtsied and turned on her heel in a hasty escape before her mortification could make an entrance. This was not going to plan. She'd expected this to be easy. But the task was far from it.

"Mama," she lamented, a shaky hand covering her mouth the moment they ducked behind a pillar.

"All will be well," her mother reassured, rubbing her arm encouragingly. "We will get through this. Together. If not him, we will find someone else—"

"I don't want anyone else." She couldn't imagine raising a child with a man who wasn't the father. Tricking someone like that… It left a sour taste in her mouth. "It has to be him." She stole her mother's fan, as Edward still held hers, and fanned her face to attempt to dry her damp eyes. "What will we do?"

Her mother fixed the broach on her bodice as they both glanced in Edward's direction. "We planted the seeds. Now we must let them grow."

"What is wrong with you?" Tobie laughed, smacking Edward in the shoulder. "She was making eyes at you and you stood there like an idiotic fool."

"She's the king's niece," he answered in a daze, staring at her fan he still held in his hand, not quite believing what just transpired. "The warlord's daughter."

"And?" Charles shoved him in the direction Vivienne had disappeared, but he dug in his feet. "Go talk to her."

Edward shook his head, rounding on his friends as he hissed, "We explored the gothic estate together. During the masquerade." When he only received blank looks, he emphasized, "We *explored* it."

"Oh, Edward…" Ivette shook her head sympathetically.

"By the heavens…" Barnaby tsked as he tipped Edward's chin up and patted his neck. "You've done it now. You're going to lose your head."

He placed a hand over his throat, imagining a sharp, steel sword beheading him for deflowering the princess. Well, he was almost certain he wasn't the one to do the job in the first place, but all the same…

"I can't see her again." He backed up, a feeling of wrongness climbing his body as his heart acted up like it always did before an episode. A sharp pain exploded through his head. His palms became cold and clammy.

Cedric took several steps forward, but Edward held up a hand to stop him. He didn't want to make a scene. He could control this. He *could*.

The conversation continued without him, the others oblivious to his struggles. Tobie said, "I thought she was still a child."

Barnaby shook his head. "She came of age a few months ago. At least her age can't count against you, Edward."

His stomach twisted uncomfortably. "I'm going to be sick."

"Not on my shoes." Barnaby stepped backward and fixed his sleeves. "Edward, you are of good breeding and in good standing with the king. Sure, you're no prince… But sometimes even princesses will marry beneath them."

"I. Cannot. Marry. Her."

For many reasons. First, he was terrified of the woman's father. Second, his sister would never allow it. Third, if Vivienne—his dear childhood friend—discovered just how weak he was, she would run for the hills.

Charles crossed his arms, staring at him with an intense expression. "Did you not stop to think of the consequences?"

Edward pressed a hand against his stomach in an attempt to quell his queasiness. "I wasn't thinking at all. Besides, I didn't know who she was. Or I would never have..." He trailed off when bile climbed his throat.

"Who else knows? Do her parents?"

He gave his friend a pointed look. "I'm quite certain I would have been killed in my sleep by now if someone else knew. I don't think she's told anyone."

Barnaby squeezed his shoulder. "Breathe, Edward. You threw this ball to find her. And now you have."

"But I never realized...I didn't..." He struggled for air, but he fought through the episode lying in wait with clawed fingers.

By the bellows of autumntide, he'd made a mistake. All he'd wanted was to be free for a single night. To be better. Stronger. He'd fallen for Vivienne rather quickly, easily taken by her humor and her wit, her adventurous spirit. One thing had happened after another, and now the real world had caught up to him.

Vivienne Winfield was the last person he should have ever dallied with. Why did he have to pick up her shoe?

"What do I do?" he breathed, slowly losing capacity in his lungs to draw in air. He fought through it.

Emmaline, Charles' wife, answered this time, a performer who had the most beautiful singing voice. "Perhaps you ought to make it right with her. Whatever that looks like."

Braving the fear running rampant through his body, he lifted his head and searched the ballroom for Vivienne. He found her on the opposite side of the room with her mother, fawned over by men and women alike. The beautiful woman laughed at something the duke said and batted her eyes at the man.

A pit of jealousy grew in his chest, starting as a small pebble and enlarging to the size of a boulder. The duke was twice her age, but he had already lost two wives and had yet to have an heir. He was likely looking for a new wife.

Edward hadn't realized he'd started stalking toward them until he'd taken several steps away from his friends. But then the feeling of wrongness smashed into him with a vengeance. Air struggled in and out of his lungs. His legs became weak.

Within moments, Cedric grabbed Edward's arm and draped it around his shoulders, pulling him swiftly out of the room until they were out of sight. He lowered him onto a cushioned bench beside large glass windows overlooking the expansive lawn below.

Edward placed one hand over his racing heart, and the other pinched the bridge of his nose to ward off the growing ache. With controlled breaths, he took each inhale and exhale slowly until his pulse slowed and his lungs ceased spasming.

He sighed as he rested his head on the glass and closed his eyes, both hating and appreciating the silence in the hallway.

Silence…

It was a constant, lonely companion. Was he destined to live out the rest of his days as a bachelor? No woman would look twice at him if they learned of the truth.

Including Vivienne.

Perhaps he should let the duke snatch her from beneath his nose.

"Am I destined to die like this?" Edward mumbled miserably to the reflection of Cedric through the glass.

Cedric tipped his head to the side and gave him a sympathetic smile. "The doctor said you wouldn't live past your fifth birthday. I think you have many years left to *live*. It is your choice how those years are lived."

"Is it, though?"

The servant remained silent. No, not a servant. His *friend*. Barnaby, Tobie, and Charles were his friends. However, they knew very little of the burdens he shouldered. But Cedric? He was there for him every day to help him when in need. He understood him, at least to some degree. Perhaps Edward would have died long ago without Cedric's care and attention. And though their relationship was…somewhere between servant and friend, he'd never been closer to anyone.

Except Vivienne…

He released a long breath and stared out the window at the peaceful pines surrounding his property. Those years of his childhood were some of his most treasured memories. He'd been struggling at the time with his health. And Vivienne? Although several years younger than him, she'd brought back the light, the life, and the laughter into an otherwise dreary world.

A faint smile lifted on his lips as he recalled all the trees they'd climbed together. Or on more difficult health days, they'd fished out on the lake behind the estate. They'd gone on adventures through the forest, collecting pine needles and leaves to make bird nests or stealing trowels from the shed and digging as deep as they dared in search of the other side of the world.

How many times had they snuck pastries from the kitchen? He remembered taking those pastries and holing up in the attic, drawing the entirety of their imaginations on parchment and hanging them about the walls.

They'd gone on countless adventures. And it had broken his heart and soul when his parents had died on their voyage and Vivienne had stopped coming to his home.

At the masquerade, he hadn't recognized her, as Vivienne Winfield had been a child in his mind at the time. But she was a beautiful, spirited young woman now with long, luscious hair and the most flattering curves…

He ran a hand over his mouth as he reminded himself how they'd made love in a vacant carriage. His childhood friend. The king's niece. The warlord's daughter.

I'm a dead man.

"Will you be returning to the party, milord?" Cedric asked, hands held behind his back as he awaited his answer.

And run away with my tail between my legs?

But he couldn't face her again. He just…didn't know how.

It was best if he maintained his distance. Because he was sick. He would always be sick. And she deserved someone healthy in her life. Even if the man was twice her age.

"Please send my regrets to my friends," he said quietly, using the wall to help him stand on wobbly feet. He squeezed his eyes shut when his surroundings spun. Despite his best efforts, he could not remain a good host for a second longer. Clara would have to play the part for the rest of the night.

Without another word, he retreated to the safety of his tower.

With a look of regret, Cedric closed the door. And locked him inside.

Chapter Six

If Edward was anything, it was *not* a person who thrilled in the rise of the sun, in the arrival of a new dawn. He preferred staying up late reading books or looking at the stars. But he most certainly shied away from the bright light of the sunrise, especially as it smashed into him the moment he stepped foot downstairs the next morning.

Cedric followed several steps behind him. Over the years, Edward had grown used to his shadowing presence. And unfortunately, more than once, Edward had had need of it.

But today? He felt stronger than he had in a while. Perhaps he ought to spend the time outdoors while he still could before winter—

He paused in his step as he entered the dining room. Light spilled over an unexpected presence sitting at the far end of the table. Nearest the window. Next to his sister.

Edward's eyes nearly bulged out of his head. His breath faltered in his lungs. The world seemed to tip upside down and almost spilled him on the floor.

He grabbed onto the back of a chair as a shaky exhale left his lips, and he couldn't help but stare back at a pair of dark brown eyes as they leveled their mischievous, amused gaze on him.

"Lady Vivienne," Edward choked, his attention dropping to the playful smirk at the edge of her lips. "What…? Why…?"

Oh, she was impossibly more beautiful than even yesterday. Full brown hair cascaded over her shoulders. A velvety green gown hugged her body in all the right places. And her eyes… Lovely. Captivating. Alluring.

"I do regret that my mother has fallen ill and cannot find the strength to journey home." Vivienne reached across the table and squeezed his sister's hand. "Clara has been most generous by allowing us to stay the night."

"You stayed the night?" he spluttered. "Why was I not informed?"

Clara rolled her eyes. "Don't mind him. His opinion is worthless in estate matters such as these. You and your mother are most welcome."

Edward's lips thinned at the embarrassing slight, though he took heart in knowing someone else was in the room, and Clara would be on her best behavior. "Then I will take myself and my worthless opinions elsewhere." He gathered several scones and pieces of cheese on a plate and retreated from the room. With a hurried step, he crossed the estate, unlocked his study, and ducked inside, hearing Cedric follow behind.

But when he turned, rather than finding Cedric's constant presence, his stomach tightened when he found Vivienne instead. His heart misbehaved, fluttering inside his chest. Breathing became difficult for the most wonderful reasons.

At least until he recovered from his shock enough to respond with panic. "Why are you here?" he hissed, glancing out the door only to find Cedric across the hallway with his back turned to them and Clara nowhere in sight. "You can't be here."

"I forgot something from my room," she replied with that mischievous smile on her face.

"No, not *here*." He gestured to his office. "Why are you in my home?"

"And why not?"

"Why not?" he spluttered. "You know why. We can't be doing this. This is a bad idea."

"What exactly do you mean by *this*, Edward?"

Her mouth curved up in a sultry grin as she ran a finger down the length of his chest. Heat spiked in his body in response to her touch. He couldn't bring himself to pull away. He didn't want to despite knowing he should.

And then she lowered her voice, her eyes sparking playfully. "I found you in the real world. And I am quite surprised we didn't run into each other before now." Her gaze passed over his face, and her expression softened. "You look nothing like I remember you."

"I can say the same about you, Vivi."

How much time had passed? Six? Seven years?

"Lady Vivienne?" his sister called somewhere down the hall, and his feet froze to the floor. "I do look forward to that carriage ride. I feel a bitter storm brewing in the air, and it may be our last opportunity."

Before he could protest, Vivienne latched onto his arm and pulled him out of the study just as his sister rounded the corner. Upon seeing the two of them, Clara's lips thinned with disapproval and disdain. The sight curled his stomach. Clara would likely seek him out later to punish him.

He tried to pull his arm out of Vivienne's grip, but she held tight and smiled at Clara, saying, "Lord Beaumont has agreed to accompany us. How enjoyable will it be to catch up with both of you?"

Clara returned a tight smile. "Indeed."

The moment his sister turned her back to them, Edward elbowed Vivienne in the ribs. She elbowed him right back before pasting on a smile when Clara glanced over her shoulder.

Fear wormed its way into his chest as he stared at his sister while gathering a warm coat and shoes for the outing. What was she going to do to him? How would he be punished? Would she lock him in his room without supper for a day or two? Would she prevent him from seeing his friends for several weeks? Would she raise a hand to strike him?

Worry over his fate successfully distracted him as he waited outside with the others in the chilly air as the servants readied the topless carriage. A frosty breath escaped his lips, the chill nipping at every exposed piece of skin.

He didn't mind the cold. Actually, he rather enjoyed it when it offered fresh air and a lively nip to the skies.

After the carriage rounded the estate, he climbed in first, scooting to the farthest side of the bench. Clara sat directly in the middle, clearly meaning for Vivienne to take up the seat on her other side to separate them and to make speaking to one another difficult.

What he hadn't expected was for Vivienne to climb the steps into the carriage and forcefully wedge herself between the two of them until Clara was compelled to scoot over.

Edward rested his mouth in his hand to hide the grin breaking free from his careful reserve. He'd forgotten how...*abrasive* Vivienne could be. If she wanted something, she wasn't the kind of person to allow others to trod over her. He'd always admired her determined attitude in every facet of her life.

It seemed as if she hadn't changed much.

As the carriage rolled forward, Edward was hyperaware of the brush of Vivienne's shoulder, of the tip of her shoe resting against his, of her scarf pooling over his upper thigh. He tried to ignore it by turning his attention to the passing scenery as the women talked, fully expecting to be snubbed.

Which was why his heart gave a start as Vivienne turned to him and animatedly spoke of her excitement over the winter markets coming to town any day now. His breath hitched as she rested one of her knees against his, stealing his thoughts from his mind and making him unable to think clearly.

"I bought the most beautiful scarf from the winter market a few years back," Vivienne continued as she took her current scarf from her own neck and draped it over his, flipping it around his neck like a warm embrace. "It has the most intricate beaded work done by the northern mountain villagers. I can barely bring myself to wear it, I love it so much."

"Is that not the point?" he asked with a raised eyebrow. "A book is not well-loved unless it's nearly falling apart."

Clara scoffed. "No one wants to hear about your books, Edward." She leaned closer to Vivienne and murmured, "Don't mind him. He's frightfully boring." And quickly, she changed the subject to frilly things like ribbons and bows and gossip.

He sighed and rested his chin in his hand, returning his attention toward the turning landscape. Only a few brown leaves remained on bare trees, waiting for the next windy breeze to pluck them from their home and take them on a flight through the kingdom.

He related all too much with the lone leaves, stuck in one place and unable to explore the world. Slowly dying until it waited to take its last breath.

"Right Edward?" Vivienne asked, snapping his attention back to her. He needn't ask for clarification when she spoke again. "I do enjoy a good book. Remember when we took the largest volume of fairy tales to our secret hideout when we were children?" The woman giggled behind a gloved hand. "You read stories in the most captivating way."

Edward laughed as he recalled the fun adventures they'd had within the pages of a book. There had never been a dull moment that passed between them. He'd missed their friendship. Immensely. "I rather enjoyed your attempts at creating the characters' voices. Especially little frog prince."

"Oh dear." She chuckled again. "I have not attempted the feat in many years."

Clara cleared her throat loudly before speaking to the driver. "I fear I am growing far too cold for such an outing. Let us return home for a warm spot of tea."

With a single nod, the driver found a place to turn around, and all too soon, they headed back toward the estate.

Disappointment rushed through Edward at having their excursion cut short. His shoulders slumped. A sigh escaped his lips. He loved the outdoors. But it wasn't often that Clara would allow him to leave the house. In fact, he'd been able to leave far less than usual lately, especially after the terrible episode he'd experienced weeks ago.

"Tis no matter," Vivienne said with a nonchalant wave of her hand. "There is plenty to do indoors. How about a game?"

Before he managed an answer, Clara cut in, "Oh, that sounds lovely. I think it's just what we need."

"Edward?"

Behind Vivienne, Clara nearly imperceptibly shook her head, a warning flashing in her eyes. If the punishment for this excursion was going to be bad, the consequence for defying her would be worse.

"I…umm…" He swallowed as he returned his gaze to Vivienne, trying to hide the fear swirling in his gut. "I have a lot of work to do. Perhaps another time."

"Oh." The disappointment in her own eyes cracked his heart. Maybe she missed his friendship just as much as he missed hers. "Yes, perhaps another time."

And then she turned back to his sister and spoke about the frilly things Clara enjoyed, all while both ignored him entirely. A cold loneliness crawled into the very foundation of his bones, an aching melancholy slowly turning his blood to stone.

Edward had been living a silly dream. What did he think would happen once he found the woman in the mask? That they would marry and live happily ever after? The sick man was never the hero in fairy tales. He was usually the sibling that ended up dying while his brother or sister lived happily ever after.

To hide his emotions, he forced himself to adopt a stone mask, to make it seem like he wasn't heartbroken in the slightest. But even then, he hugged Vivienne's scarf a little closer, breathing in her scent wafting from the soft fabric. She smelled like flowery perfume, and it brought him back to the night everything had changed between them. Back to laughter and happiness and carefree love.

The horses halted too quickly, causing him to hit the side of the carriage. Vivienne stumbled into him, latching onto him for balance. When she turned her head toward him, she ensnared him with her beautiful brown eyes.

All of his surroundings faded away. The sounds melted until he only heard his own heartbeat pulsing through his ears and her short breaths escaping pretty pink lips. Every place they touched set him ablaze, and he found himself craving her company more than he'd wanted anything in the world.

"Apologies!" the driver called out, effectively breaking the spell between them.

Before his sister had a chance to catch them in that position, Edward pulled her scarf from around his neck and draped it over hers.

"Save a book for me," she whispered. "Perhaps you might allow me to read quietly in the corner while you work."

He didn't get the chance to reply when Clara turned toward them, and he quickly placed distance between Vivienne and himself.

Without a word, he bowed to them and hurried into the estate, trying to escape Clara before she intercepted him. She wouldn't dare harm him with guests in the house. Would she?

Still, he increased his pace across the estate, up the flight of stairs leading to his room, and closed the door behind him. He could not hide from her. He knew that. But he could certainly try.

After several minutes, he relaxed when he thought she might not follow him to his room. He released a melancholy sigh as he took off his coat and shoes before sitting on the edge of his bed. There was no use lamenting over his fate. He was no hero in a storybook. No matter how much he wished to be.

The door opened suddenly, and he lifted his head, expecting to find Cedric. But then his throat constricted with fear when his sister entered instead. "Clara."

But she simply smiled rather than charging at him with a raised hand. "I noticed you've been a bit sluggish lately, and I wanted to check on you myself." She placed a vial of his medicine in his hand. "I so desperately want you to get better, Eddie. I planned an outing with the queen after the storm abates, and I do hope you might be able to join us."

"The queen?"

Clara had always aspired to fit in with such a crowd, but she'd never once tried to include him.

She nodded, and when he didn't drink his medicine, she unstopped the vial for him and handed it back. "Little James is so excited to visit the palace. Imagine that! The king's sister invited us herself. She's still feeling ill, but when she recovers, she would love to have us."

Edward fingered the vial, staring at the yellowish contents within. Perhaps if he felt well enough to go… Would Vivienne be there?

The thought of her gave him enough motivation to place the vial to his lips and drink. If he continued to take his medicine, could he possibly get better? Could he become strong enough to reenter society and somehow woo Vivienne?

If he made a connection with her, it would be advantageous for his sister as well, considering she aspired to belong to the queen's close-knit group.

His sister took the vial back from him, the smile lingering on her face. He blinked heavily when a sudden fatigue pressed down on his shoulders. He hadn't gotten enough sleep the night before, as thoughts of Vivienne had plagued his mind.

Unable to hold his head upright, he curled up on his bed, but the fatigue only seemed to grow when his mind spun dizzily, and his eyelids felt as if they were weighted with bricks.

Clara tucked blankets around him before opening the door, turning back to him one last time with a smile on her face. "Oh, you poor thing. Sweet dreams."

Finally, the fatigue dragged him into cool waters, and his entire world turned dark.

Chapter Seven

"Forgive my tardiness," Clara said as she entered the room in a swoosh of skirts, a bright smile on her face. "I was seeing to my brother. The poor thing must have contracted something at the party last night, as he's feeling under the weather."

A frown pulled on Vivienne's lips as her gaze darted toward the door as if she might find Edward entering the room at any moment. But he didn't. Instead, a servant entered with tea and light refreshments.

"He seemed fine during the carriage ride," she replied distractedly, rising from her chair and wandering across the room until she stared out into the hallway. Edward was nowhere within sight.

"He's asleep." Clara lifted a teapot and poured two cups of tea. "Out like a light when I went to check on him." She smiled reassuringly. "I'm sure he'll feel well enough to join us tomorrow."

Are you avoiding me? she wondered silently. Of course, she'd taken him off guard by staying the night in his home. But...

She forced herself to keep her hand by her side rather than stray to her belly. The outside of her lower stomach felt harder now. She could feel the baby growing inside her, not to mention the constant nausea plaguing her relentlessly.

Panic nipped at her pulse, causing it to thrum faster in her veins. Charming Edward was proving more difficult than she thought. She liked him. By the kingdom's waters, she liked him a lot. And her feelings terrified her. Because she might have to marry the duke instead.

The thought churned her stomach until bile climbed her throat. She didn't know what to do. If their child was forced to live without its father?

"Lady Vivienne," Clara said, pulling her back to the present. "Might I suggest we find a relaxing activity to occupy our time?"

Finally, she tore her attention away from the hallway and forced a smile to her face. "Of course."

The next hours were filled with games, embroidery, and music, and each moment spent in the quiet stillness spiraled her farther and farther down her hole of worry. She perked up at every sound within the estate, hoping to hear Edward's voice or eavesdrop on a servant speaking about him in hushed whispers.

But there was nothing. It was as if he suddenly didn't exist.

After supper, she excused herself and tried her hardest not to flee from Clara's constant presence and toward the safety of her room. But rather than disappearing behind her door, she knocked abruptly on her mother's door and slipped inside.

A lantern lit up her mother's bored expression from where she lay in her bed with her embroidery in her lap. Although her eyes lit up as if she were silently relieved for her company, she maintained the proper poise of a woman of good breeding.

Realizing they were alone, Vivienne moodily kicked off her shoes and loosened her corset. The lack of pressure against her belly gave her some measure of relief. At least until she could no longer hold herself back and ran for the chamber pot, making it just in time to vomit inside.

"Oh, Vivienne," her mother murmured sympathetically, and when she climbed onto the bed and rested her head on her mother's lap, her mother stroked her hair in a comforting manner. "I remember my first pregnancy. It was misery. I can't imagine having to hide it."

"Why are you being so nice to me?" she asked, her voice muffled by the bedspread. "I imagined you to be angrier."

"I've made my fair share of mistakes, too. I only wish my mother had been kind enough to help me through the worst of them. I could not fathom spurning you for being human." And then her mother sighed. "Feigning illness is far more dreadful at someone else's home than my own." She chuckled and shook her head. "How did things go with Lord Beaumont today?"

"Terribly! I know he is attracted to me. I can see it in his eyes. He likes it when I touch him. But something is holding him back. He wants nothing to do with me."

"You mustn't give up." Her mother continued to gently stroke her hair. "Men are not so complicated that a pretty face can't hold them captive."

Silent, angry sobs wracked her frame. "All this time, he has not bothered to search for me. He literally lives down the street!" Well, thirty minutes down the street by carriage was close enough.

Despite her outburst, her mother continued her calm administration. "Some men are harder to catch than others. You must keep trying. It's not always easy."

"What more can I do?"

"Well..." Her mother released a long breath, which managed to rattle the flame of her lantern sitting at her bedside. "You either try harder or find an easier man to catch. The duke—"

"Try harder?" she squeaked. "I have been trying my hardest to catch the man's eye. Clara keeps ruining it."

She got the distinct impression Clara was interfering on purpose, though she couldn't fathom why.

Her mother took a deep breath and tried again. "The duke has asked for your hand, Vivienne."

The breath whooshed from her lungs, and she shot up to a sitting position to stare at her mother. "Pardon?"

"At the ball last night. Your father arrived near the end. And the duke asked for your hand in marriage."

Vivienne covered her face with her hand, a shuddering breath escaping her lungs. Denying a duke simply wasn't done. She'd feared this would happen. And like she'd expected, her heart began to shatter piece by piece.

"What day can I expect to be married off to the oaf?" She bit her tongue until it bled, keeping herself from saying anything more. The duke was a kind man, she knew that. But he was also old enough to be her father.

After a moment's silence, she felt her mother's soft hand on the top of her head. Her reassuring touch was enough for her to lift her head to view her mother's concerned gaze through blurry, tear-filled eyes.

"Your father has left the matchmaking to me." The stroke of her fingers helped calm her melancholy heart. "I told the duke that you are still young. That he must first woo you until you accept his hand. It gives you more time to charm your viscount while still keeping the duke's offer on the table."

Emotion crashed into her as she threw her arms around her mother's neck. "Thank you. I will try my hardest."

Her mother scoffed, rolling her eyes. "I can hardly believe you've had to try so hard with Lord Beaumont to begin with. Does he not have eyes?"

She laugh-sobbed as she dried her tears with a swipe of her sleeve. "I will try harder. How long can you pretend illness?"

"A few days more at most. I'm the sickest I've ever been, remember?"

Again, she laughed, grateful for her mother's support. "What would I do without you?"

"Just don't cause a scandal," her mother warned. "It's hard enough to cover up this mess as it is."

"I promise I won't." Or at least she planned to not get caught where she wasn't supposed to be. Tomorrow, she would succeed at reeling Edward in.

But as tomorrow came and went, her distress only continued to grow as she paced her room, paced the drawing room, and paced the hallways in search of any sign of Edward. After inquiring of his absence, one of the servants confirmed he had been terribly sick and was sequestered in his room.

Not only sick…

But after laying her charms on the flustered servant, she learned Edward had not yet woken from the day before. And when two days became three, her distress transitioned from fear for herself and her condition to fear for *him*. The servant once more said he still had not woken. But three days?

Was he truly asleep? Or still avoiding her?

Deciding to take matters into her own hands, she lit a lantern and snuck through the darkened house when everyone was asleep, wearing a green cloak on top of her nightgown and thin slippers over her stockinged feet.

She placed one foot on the stone staircase leading to Edward's tower, and hearing nothing coming from either direction, she began her silent climb up the stairs.

The chilly stone seeped through her slippers. A frosty breath escaped her mouth. But she shoved away the mild discomfort and replaced it with raw determination to get to the bottom of whatever was going on.

She slowed her steps at the top of the dark stairwell, her eyes widening to find his door closed. Alarm slammed into her chest when she spotted a lock keeping his door shut from the *outside*.

With hurried steps, she raced up the remaining stairs, grabbed the lock, and pulled. It didn't give in the slightest, locking Edward inside.

Glancing down the stairs to find herself alone, she rapped softly on his door, but no sound came from within. Could he truly be inside? Would someone be so cruel as to keep someone so important in society as a prisoner in his own home?

"I must be mistaken," she whispered to placate herself. "This isn't the correct door. It must be a broom closet."

But then something dropped to the floor on the opposite side of the door. Panic clawed at her heart as she rapped louder on the worn wood, wincing when the soft bangs echoed down the stairwell.

No answer.

Vivienne picked up her skirts and dashed down the stairs. Despite her thin clothing and even thinner slippers, she gave no thought for herself as she threw open the front doors of the estate and escaped outside. A chill wind from a late-autumn night seeped into her bones. Snowflakes fell on her hair and eyelashes. But despite the bite of the air, she glanced around her to make sure she was alone before rushing along the estate at a brisk pace. Only when she reached the base of the tower did she halt in her steps, breathing heavily.

The tower window was dark, not a single flicker of candlelight or a silhouette to draw her attention. Her panic consumed her, worry for her friend driving her into sifting through the light powder of snow at her feet with her hands.

Her numb fingers closed around a rock. And taking aim, she lobbed it toward the window.

Plink!

Edward sluggishly pulled himself out of sleep, blinking in confusion as he stared up at the darkness of his ceiling. When had he fallen asleep? He remembered going on a carriage ride through the countryside. Vivienne's warm laughter. Her knee resting against his.

He vaguely recalled Clara acting kindly toward him, but then...

Scratching his chin, he struggled to recall anything after his sister had visited his chambers. He must have fallen asleep.

Plink!

The sound startled him upright, and his gaze darted back and forth across his room. Reaching for the tinderbox on his bedside table, he struck it with the flint and lit his lantern, frowning when he found himself in looser and more comfortable clothing than what he'd worn earlier.

Plink!

Finally, he located the sound coming from something small hitting the glass of his window. Setting his lantern down on his desk, he opened his windows and flinched when a cold draft entered the room.

"Edward!" someone hissed.

He squinted against his sleepy confusion and located a white and green speck down below. He blinked several times until the image came together to form the silhouette of a woman wearing a nightgown, her feet in threadbare slippers and a green cloak over her shoulders.

Alertness flooded through him when he recognized Vivienne. He quickly smoothed down his hair and clothing before peering farther over the side of the stone ledge.

"Vivi!" he hissed as he glanced back and forth across the yard. His tower wasn't within the vantage point of the rest of the estate, and no one else lingered outside. "What are you doing? What hour is it?"

She held a hand to her heart and visibly took a deep breath. "I thought you were dead up there!" she squeaked. "I was so worried."

He frowned. "Why in heaven's name would you think me dead?"

"You've been in there for several days."

The blood rushed out of his face, and his body took on a chill unrelated to the cold night. The sudden hunger and thirst running rampant through him gave away the fact that he likely hadn't eaten anything substantial in a long while.

"Why is your bedroom door locked from the outside?" she asked in a watery tone, snapping his attention back to her. "Are you in trouble, Edward?"

He blinked several times to try to make sense of the situation through his still-foggy mind. Was this due to his condition? True, it had become worse in the past year alone. But never this bad.

"I'm coming up," she declared as she grabbed stone after stone, somehow finding a foothold in the towering structure.

"Stop!" he gasped. "You will injure yourself."

Thankfully, she lowered herself back to the ground, only to stare up at him with hands resting over her hips. "Edward!" she hissed in the darkness. "Let down a rope!"

"Are you daft?" he hissed right back. "You're not climbing the wall. Besides, you can't possibly be strong enough."

She planted her fists on her hips. "I'm plenty strong enough. I wasn't built daintily like the rest of the females at court, my father always says." Shaking her head, she gave him a pointed stare. "I can either do this with a rope or without. The choice is yours."

"I don't have a rope."

Her teasing smile quirked to the side. "Let down your hair?"

He rolled his eyes and scoffed. "It's not *that* long. Besides, you quite liked the length all those weeks ago."

His ears burned with fluster after mentioning the one thing he swore he would put behind him. But it was difficult when that night together was seared into his brain in the most pleasant way.

"Mmhmm," she confirmed in a sing-song voice. But then she moved as if to climb the wall again.

"Wait!"

He rushed back into his room, his gaze darting about as he tried to find something to use for her to climb. When he found no such rope like he thought he wouldn't, he quickly stripped the sheets from his bed and tied two of them together, testing the knot before throwing it over the window sill and down as far as it would reach. It dangled near the top of her head, but she still managed to grab a hold of it.

Using all the strength he possessed, he held onto the other end and prayed to the Mother Goddess that it wouldn't rip. He even braced one of his legs against the wall to prevent his own weight from slipping.

"What am I doing?" he chastised himself. Allowing a woman to climb a wall into his bedroom in the dead of night? She could injure herself for one. For two, it was vastly inappropriate.

Just when he felt the urge to glance over the side of the sill, Vivienne's head crested the top of the ledge. He rushed forward to help by grabbing her securely around the waist and heaving her over.

He misjudged his strength, or perhaps her weight, as he stumbled backward with her in his arms until they crashed to the ground, sprawled out in a tangle of limbs. He hadn't the strength to do anything other than lie with his arms on either side of him, staring at the ceiling as the world spun.

His condition truly *was* getting worse. What was he to do? The doctor had said there was no cure for this save for a risky operation.

"Edward?" Vivienne gasped, scrambling into a sitting position with her legs straddling his waist as she cradled his face in her hands.

"I'm well, just dazed," he grunted as he pushed himself to sitting, only to find himself far too close to her for comfort, the two of them nearly nose to nose. This was…dangerous. This could not happen again. He would accept her friendship but nothing more. Not this time.

No matter how much he longed for something more.

He stood, facing his back to her as he retrieved the lantern and set it on the center of the floor to illuminate more of their surroundings.

"Care to answer my questions?" she asked, hands on her hips again.

He tried to hide his grin at her idea of a confrontation. It was so like Vivienne to make it as extreme as possible. "I don't have all the answers. But I assume since you went through all the effort… You're here to play?"

Even in the darkness, he noticed the color rising to her cheeks.

"Play?" she asked breathlessly.

Happiness bloomed in his chest by simply being in her presence as he crossed his room and threw open the doors of a floor-to-ceiling cabinet stuffed to the brim with rows of books, games, and a variety of musical instruments. More books were hidden beneath his bed, but he decided not to overwhelm her too much.

"Name your pick."

He watched as she approached the cabinet with a curious expression, her strong but feminine fingers trailing over the spines of his books, almost reverently.

"Read me a story." She glanced up from her perusing and met his eye in the dim light. "Just like when we were children."

A smile lifted on his lips as he threw aside one of his pillows to grab the very same fairy tale book they'd read countless times as children. The spine hung by a thread, and numerous pages had come loose from the binding, only kept in place by pure determination and a little bit of luck.

"According to you..." She laid out a blanket on the ground and set the lantern directly in the middle. "That is an extremely well-loved book."

"Oh, it is. I read it often."

"Why?"

But he didn't answer her question as he snatched the comforter from atop his bed and threw it over the both of them, trapping them inside a dark tent illuminated by a single lantern. The candle cast shadows across Vivienne's face and flickered as it threatened to give out. But there was just enough air to give it life. Just enough to keep it burning.

Vivienne giggled as she scooted closer until her foot rested against his leg. He should have pulled away, to place distance between them. But he was so lonely. And even the small touch made him feel not quite so alone anymore.

It was pathetic. He already knew that. But for just a short time, he could enjoy her company.

If they didn't take it too far like last time.

Edward cleared his throat, giving her a serious stare as he opened to a well-worn page in the book. But then he broke out a silly voice as he read the first line.

Vivienne fell over in stitches, laughter erupting from her mouth. And when he read the next few lines, her laughter only grew louder.

"Shh!" he hissed, a grin spread across his face as he pressed his finger to her lips. "Someone will hear you, and your climb up the wall will all be for naught."

"All right, all right." She took a deep breath and straightened her spine. "You make me laugh too much. I will read it."

But as she carefully took the book from him, she deepened her voice and made a hilariously comical face. The moment she read the next line, *he* broke into laughter, holding his stomach when he could not keep his amusement contained.

"Hush!" she hissed right back, now placing a finger against *his* lips. But it didn't quite have the same effect. Because his stomach fluttered, and his heart skipped, and her beautiful brown gaze held him captive. They were not the same people as they had been years ago. No longer children. No longer innocent of the world. Yet at the same time, their friendship remained. Playful. Optimistic. Easy. But with an underlying emotion tying their souls tightly together.

"This is a bad idea," he voiced out loud, not for the first time. "You shouldn't be here."

"And what is so wrong with my company?" she huffed, dropping her hand and giving him an adorable pout. "Am I so unbearable to be around?"

"It's not your company I'm concerned about." He threw his arms up as much as he could when confined beneath the sheet. "Your father is going to murder me. You have to go."

"I *knew* you were scared of my father. Is that all it is?"

He pressed his lips together, saying no more. He felt torn in every direction between what he wanted, his fear of others, and the certainty that she would never choose him if she learned the truth about him.

Her voice cracked. "I need to know you are all right. I am concerned about you. I'm terrified that if I leave this tower, I won't see you again."

"Vivi..." he murmured. The declaration of her concern warmed his heart in ways he didn't know he could experience. The selfish part of him refused to let go. At least for now. Tomorrow, he would fight against his unrealistic dreams again. But tonight, he couldn't bring himself to raise the sword.

Without another word of argument, he took the book of fairy tales back and settled it over his lap. "No more giggling," he warned, pointing a finger at her.

She locked her lips closed. "I will be quiet as a mouse."

He began reading from the book once more, this time keeping his silly voices at a minimum. Until the candle flickered out, and the two of them drifted off to sleep side by side on the floor as if they were children again.

And for a single moment, he was happier than he'd been in a very long time.

Chapter Eight

Vivienne was up to her neck in hot water.

Which could be a good thing, considering her circumstances, but it was also terribly bad. Because she did not want to cause her family scandal. And nothing could be more scandalous than waking up in a man's arms. In his house. In his *room*. Wearing nothing more than her nightgown to provide her modesty.

But at the same time, she enjoyed how Edward's pleasant heat seeped into her back. How his long, steady breaths caressed her ear with each exhale. How his strong arm lay draped over her waist, giving her a sense of safety and protection.

At least, she enjoyed it until her stomach heaved violently. This time, she could not keep it down as she launched to her feet, sprinted across the room, and threw the windows open before she retched over the sill.

When she finished, embarrassment climbed into her cheeks in the form of a heated blush as she turned to face Edward, a hand over her mouth.

He stumbled to his feet, his hair splayed in all directions, and a crease of worry between his eyebrows. "Are you all right?" he mumbled. "Shall I fetch a doctor?"

"In your room, Edward?"

After a sweeping glance around himself, he swore. "This is not good. We were not supposed to fall asleep." But then his worry returned, momentarily replacing the panic. "Are you ill?"

For a long moment, she stared back at him, wanting to tell him the truth. He deserved to know. It was only fair. It was only right. Surely, he would understand just how dire her situation was.

But her mother's counsel echoed in her mind. *"No one, and I repeat no one, is to hear of what you just told me. Not even the father of this child."*

Edward had made it abundantly clear that he didn't mean to pursue a relationship with her despite her hopes to sway his mind. If she told him of the child, she would be forcing his hand. To either marry her when he didn't want to or to abandon her and destroy their friendship.

Admittedly, she was scared. Terrified, even. His rejection of her and their child might break her.

So, she lied. Because she was too frightened to tell the truth.

"I must have caught what my mother has." She made a show of looking around the room to shift the attention away from herself, her gaze landing on the sky outside, becoming lighter with each passing minute. "I apologize. I did not mean to stay the night. Where is the rope? I must return to my chambers at once."

"I don't feel comfortable with you climbing back down the tower." He lowered his voice. "What if you fall?"

"What other way is there?" She placed her hands on her hips. "You never explained why *you* are locked in here yourself. You have conveniently avoided the topic. Edward, you can tell me anything. Are you in trouble?"

"No." He shook his head. "It's not like that."

"Then what?"

But before he could answer, the lock on the door jiggled. She inhaled sharply as Edward grabbed her around the waist and spun her until she found herself within the corner of the door just as it opened, concealing her from whomever resided on the other side.

Peering through the crack behind the door, she barely made out the silhouette of another man. A servant.

"You're awake!" the servant cried. "I was so worried. It's been three days, Eddie. Clara has been beside herself. She thought you wouldn't make it."

Edward lowered his voice. "What is going on, Cedric? I've been asleep. Nothing more. But to think me dying?"

"It happened again," Cedric replied hesitantly. "But no one could wake you."

When Edward didn't answer, the servant entered more fully into the room. Vivienne knew she should round the door quickly before someone caught her. But she needed answers, too.

"What in the nine kingdoms happened here?" Cedric asked as he picked up the comforter and blankets from the ground. "Where are your sheets?"

"I got cold," Edward lied, and she noticed him kicking a piece of firewood beneath the bed and dropping a pillow over the sheet-rope to hide them from his servant while his back was turned. "So...I burned them."

Cedric's mouth slowly fell open with blatant disbelief. "You...burned them."

"Yes."

"All of them."

"Yeeeeah." He shuffled his feet. "Sorry."

"You could have rang for me, despite the late hour. I would have brought more firewood."

"I didn't want to wake you."

Despite wanting to overhear more of the conversation, her reputation was at stake. When Cedric's attention was occupied with folding up the blankets, she slipped around the door and into the stairwell, trying to keep as silent as possible as she descended the stairs to the ground level of the estate.

Hushed whispers and clanging silverware reached her ears from around the corner. She fled in the opposite direction, glancing over her shoulder to make sure no one spotted her.

Sure, she shouldn't have stayed the night with Edward. But his voice had been so soothing. It brought back memories of some of the happiest times of her life. She'd felt safe with him, and she hadn't wanted to leave his side for a single moment.

But she'd also been careless. It wouldn't happen again.

The banging silverware and voices became more frantic behind her. Curiosity urged her to return the way she'd come. But self-preservation won out, telling her to continue forward.

She rounded the corner, only to gasp as she ran into Clara.

"Forgive me," Vivienne said, wrapping her cloak more securely around her shoulders. "I am so embarrassed about my state of undress. I went out for air and lost track of time." But when Clara's lips thinned, she hurried to change the subject. "Why are you up at such an early hour?"

Clara's attention turned toward the hallway. "I heard my brother is awake. I wanted to see for myself." The woman's careful expression crumbled, and she pulled a handkerchief from her pocket and dabbed at her eyes. "I am so afraid of losing him. I thought for sure he was leaving us and suffering me to manage the estate without him. Whatever would we do?"

Vivienne patted the other woman's shoulder, trying to offer some measure of comfort. Nothing made sense anymore. Nothing at all. Edward was well. She'd seen him herself only minutes prior.

"I'm sure he's just fine," she reassured. "Perhaps checking on him will help relieve your worries."

With a nod, Clara continued on her way.

Her pulse calming a fraction, Vivienne picked up her pace until she reached her chambers, slamming the door behind her. Her breaths quickened as she closed her eyes and leaned back against the cool stone wall.

That had been close.

She never wanted to force Edward's hand, and ruining her reputation and threatening his was a quick way for him to resent her.

Her eyes flashed open, and with determined strides, she crossed the room and threw her wardrobe open to reveal several dresses her own servants had dropped by days earlier. She sifted through fabrics consisting of green, blue, and yellow hues until her fingers brushed against a light blue gown that complimented her complexion and hugged her in all the right places.

She'd always felt lovely and feminine in this dress.

If it didn't help her catch Edward's eye, then she didn't know what would.

"Stick out your tongue," Doctor Greaves instructed, and Edward nearly gagged on the stick he placed at the back of his throat.

The man's mouth pinched, his eyes hardening as he finished the examination by checking his pulse. "I won't lie to you," he said, finally sitting straight in his chair and lifting his gaze. "Your condition has worsened. I cannot guarantee you will last the remainder of the year."

A cold disbelief washed through Edward's veins as he stared back at the man. "There are less than three months left of the year."

"Precisely." Greaves frowned as he returned his medical equipment to his bag. "I do not like to be the bearer of bad news, Lord Beaumont. But it would be wise to create a will, if you haven't already."

Slowly, a numbness crawled up Edward's legs, his torso, and settled as ice in his chest. He barely heard Clara arguing with the doctor, saying he must be mistaken. He could hardly pay attention when his sister began sobbing, when she yelled and screamed, several servants having to hold her back from hitting the doctor.

All he managed was to stare into his lap as shock coursed through him, unable to bring himself to move a single muscle, even as Greaves packed up and left the estate.

This couldn't be the truth. Only months left to live? How could his life get cut short so suddenly? It couldn't possibly be real.

Before anyone managed to lock him back in his room, he floated numbly down the stairs, grabbed his coat from a hook in the entryway, and placed his hand on the smooth door handle of the exit.

"Edward!" Clara shouted after him, rushing into the room. He couldn't bother himself to lift his gaze when his attention remained fixed on the marble floors. "Don't you dare set foot outside. It's snowing heavily. You'll catch a chill."

"If you want to be included in the will," Edward hissed, "then you will allow me a few minutes to myself."

She didn't stop him as he flung the door open, bracing himself against a bitter, snowy wind before stalking out of the house and into the gardens around the estate. The haze of white clung to his hair, eyelashes, and clothing. It obscured his vision of the path ahead. But still, he continued forward with one foot in front of the other until he could go no farther when his heart threatened to collapse him.

He slumped onto a bench covered in white powder, uncaring about the chill nor about getting his clothing wet. His heart flipped and flopped inside his chest, the rhythm disjointed and disorienting. His head spun. His pulse raced.

The terrible sensations had often been his constant companion. But he hadn't always been prone to collapsing and sleeping days at a time. However, lately, he experienced more bad days than good.

He buried his face in his hand as emotion pricked at his eyes. There was still so much he wanted to do. So much he wanted to see and experience. He wanted to travel the kingdom. See the world. Sail distant waters. Experience life.

But he'd been locked in the blasted tower for most of his life to "keep him safe." Well, what if he didn't want to be safe? What more did it matter when he only had months left to live?

The soft crunch of snow gave away another presence. Rather than sadness, anger crashed into him. He dropped his hand and snarled at the newcomer, "I said leave me alone, Clara!"

"Edward..." a voice murmured, one definitely not belonging to his sister.

He inhaled sharply and swiped at his eyes, clearing his vision enough to view a beautiful brunette wearing a blue dress peeking out from beneath a green cloak. Vivienne stopped hesitantly several paces away, almost as if not knowing whether to approach or give him space.

"It's best if you go home," he said quietly, trying to rein his emotions back.

She gestured to the ever-growing white landscape. "In this weather? I don't think it's an option."

"Then it's best if you go inside."

"Who do you think I am, Edward?"

"The niece of a king?" he answered feebly. It was all he could do. He was so tired. Sick and tired and absolutely exhausted. His body was failing him, and there was nothing more he could do.

But she shook her head as she sat beside him on the bench, completely disregarding the masses of snow accumulated there. Her gentle hand cupped his cheek and turned his head so he stared at her distorted image through tear-filled eyes. "I am your *friend*. If you are hurting, so am I."

"We were reacquainted only recently."

"And?" She slipped her hand into his and squeezed. "Our friendship has not broken its stride. I'm here if you want to talk about whatever is ailing you. Or if you prefer not to talk…" A smile lifted on her lips, sad and heartbroken as if reflecting his sorrow. "I am told I give rather marvelous hugs."

He swallowed, trying to rein back his emotions but failing. "Vivi… In another life…"

He couldn't finish the sentence. He didn't know how. Because he longed for more than just friendship. But life was cruel. And he had no right to ask for anything more when he knew he didn't have enough time to speak vows at an altar.

Who reached for whom first? He wasn't sure. All he knew was they came together for a tight embrace. She held him as his shoulders shook silently, as tears cascaded down his face, as his heart broke for the life he would never have.

In another life, they could have been happy. But he didn't have another life. He only had this one.

When his hysterics died down, he didn't want to release her, not even at the expense that someone might peek out a window and find them in the garden together. But it was more likely the storm would obscure them anyway, providing at least a little privacy from prying eyes.

"Will you get locked in your room again tonight?" she asked as she stroked his hair, likely wet now from all the snow.

Of course, he didn't want to answer the question, especially when she was correct. She seemed to take his silence as an affirmation.

"Well, then. You can expect me to visit each day that this storm lasts, and we'll read and play games and pass the time with happy thoughts."

"Clara and other servants come up during the day."

"Then I will not be challenged by coming up during the night."

"Well... I don't know about...that." His words slowly trailed off as she turned her head and kissed his cheek. The place where her lips touched his skin warmed him from the inside out until, rather than a chill in his bones, his blood flushed with heat. He didn't often receive any form of physical affection, and he didn't realize he was touch-starved until now.

More than anything, he wanted to turn his head, to capture her lips with his. But he held himself back. It wasn't fair. To either of them. For him to mislead her into thinking they could be anything more than what they were.

"I don't want you climbing the wall," he rasped, finally finding his words.

"I won't climb it unless the storm abates. But I will visit every night."

He shook his head, staring at her in wonder. "Why would you do that for me?"

She shrugged, drawing patterns in the snow on the bench with her bare finger. "You must be awfully lonely up there. I would be, and I know you'd do the same for me." Before he could reply, she said, "My mother is feeling better today." Her change of subject threw him off guard as if she'd blindfolded him and spun him around until he didn't know what direction was where. "But I fear the storm may keep us here longer than expected." She batted her snow-frosted eyelashes at him. "Of course, if the lord of the house permits our continued occupancy."

But he only gestured to the snow billowing from the heavens and clinging to every available surface. "There is not much choice, is there?"

"Don't want our carriage to get stuck."

"You would most certainly strand yourself long before you reached home."

She tipped her head to the side. "Are you afraid of a bit of cold?"

He only lifted an eyebrow as his gaze swept across their snowy surroundings. "I'm sitting in a pile of snow. Do I look like it scares me?"

A laugh escaped her, and her hand trailed from his shoulder, down his arm, until it rested lightly over his forearm. The chill burned away entirely when her touch left heat in its wake.

"I'll come again tonight. And wear something warm just in case the storm settles."

"Why?"

"It's a surprise." Now it was her turn to lift an eyebrow. "Are you capable of climbing down a wall? Or shall I search the grounds for a ladder?"

Fatigue sat heavy on his chest, and the thought of even the smallest physical exertion exhausted him. But he didn't want her to know. If anything, he wanted the remaining few months of his life to be filled with excitement and adventure. He didn't want Vivienne to look at him with pity in her eyes.

"I'm sure I can manage a rope."

Actually, he wasn't sure at all. But he was determined to spend every moment possible with her until she had to leave…

…and he never saw her again in this life.

"Vivi…" he murmured, taking her hand in his. His mouth opened and closed as he tried to find the words, as he tried to express what her friendship meant to him. But in the end, he only dropped her hand and released a long sigh. "Tonight then."

"Tonight. Don't be late."

"I don't think that's possible."

Sure enough, true to her word, Vivienne showed up that night piled to the brim in layers of warm clothes and furs to protect her from the raging snow storm. But no matter how relentless the chill, her smile never ceased as she stood at the bottom of the tower and he at the top. They talked for hours upon hours about books and stars, about adventures and traveling, about everything and nothing.

For three nights, she came to him, lighting up his world with happiness from her conversation and her presence. Yes, he'd been touch-starved. But he'd also been starved of a good, deep friendship unlike any he'd had before. Only with Vivienne did he feel like he could be his true self, and to his delight, she seemed to like him as he was, even the parts of him Clara often claimed were boring and unnoteworthy.

His heart fell for Vivienne a little more each time she showed up after everyone had gone to bed. They were so similar with interests and dreams of the future. Someday, she wanted to travel across the kingdoms. And playfully, he promised to take her when the snow thawed.

They flirted and bantered. Laughed and smiled. All with a tower between them.

On the fourth day, the storm finally ceased, though it left a deep, untraversable build-up of snow, continuing to strand Vivienne and her mother at the estate. However, it would likely melt by tomorrow. And a part of him dreaded Vivienne leaving him and taking the colors of her world with her.

As he worked in his office, Cedric entered with a rap on the door, handing him a vial of medicine.

"What good will it do now?" He pushed it away and continued writing on the piece of parchment in front of him, a correspondence from one of his tenants asking for another month to pay their rent.

"Give you more time, perhaps?"

Edward paused his writing as he stared at the yellow contents of the vial. Whether he died in two months or six didn't make much difference in the outcome of his life. Besides, the medicine often made him sleepy. He would rather stick his hand in the fire than miss out on a single night with Vivienne.

He reached for the vial, gripping it tightly in his hand. "Will you add another log to the hearth, Cedric?"

As his servant complied, Edward uncorked the vial and quickly dumped it into the nearby potted plant before making a show of wiping his mouth with the back of his hand right as Cedric turned around.

This wasn't something he needed to hide from his friend. He knew Cedric would support him with whatever he decided. But he couldn't risk his unwillingness to consume the medicine reaching his sister's ears.

What has become of me? he silently scoffed as he pushed the empty vial to the end of the table. *I must sneak around in my own house.*

Another servant knocked on the doorframe and curtsied. "Your Lordship. The duke has just sent gifts."

"Gifts?" He pushed himself to his feet. "Where are they?"

"Well..." The woman's face blanched as she curtsied again. "They are not for you, Lord Beaumont."

"Then who are they for?"

"For Lady Vivienne."

Chapter Nine

"Oh! What is this?"

Vivienne's eyes widened with wonder as she took in the spread of jams, jellies, bread, and pastries littering nearly every available space on the table in the drawing room.

She picked up a thin, rectangle box wrapped with a small red bow. Pinching the ribbon between her fingers, she pulled, and the bow unraveled. When she opened the box, she found herself unable to hold back a gasp as she stared back at a string of rubies inlaid in gold settings.

The gems sparkled beneath the light filtering through the window. Beautiful and elegant and befitting the neck of a duchess.

Oh, it was hard to remember that the duke was a stuffy, boring man with hardly an interesting thing to say when he gave her such beautiful gifts. But no matter how much she loved the necklace, she knew she could never be happy with the man. It would be a terrible marriage.

"Please excuse me," Clara rasped, her expression crumpling as she gazed at the necklace moments before she rushed out of the room and left Vivienne alone with her mother. For several seconds, she stared after her, wondering if she'd said something to upset her.

"He also sent along this," her mother said, now downstairs after "miraculously" feeling much better after the snowstorm prevented them from returning home anyway.

Her mother handed her a letter. Vivienne broke open the seal and read out loud. "'*All the glittering jewels could never surpass your beauty. Duke Oliver Hastings.*'" She fluttered her hand to her face and pretended to swoon. "Oh, what an original love letter!" she exclaimed. "How my beauty surpasses blah blah blah."

"Vivienne Winfield!" her mother chastised. "It is a generous gift."

"It is exactly like all the rest from my other suitors!" She dropped the letter onto the table, not at all feigning disgust at the words. "Is that all I am, Mother? Beautiful? Is that all I can ever be to a man? Am I nothing more than a show horse bred for a man's pleasure?"

Again, her mother gasped, now fanning *her* face. It reminded her that Edward still had her fan, and she wondered what he had done with it.

"You are a respectable young lady, and I will not hear such words from your mouth." The other woman gestured toward the letter discarded on the table. "You will write him back, thanking him for such thoughtful gifts."

With a sigh, she held out the necklace and admired the way it sparkled. "The jewels are quite lovely. But to wear them means to accept his inevitable proposal."

"You certainly could do worse than a duke." Her mother continued to drone on about Duke Hastings' fantastic qualities, but when Vivienne heard a quiet shuffle from the hallway, her attention snapped toward the open door.

Only to find Edward staring back at her. His gaze darted from the necklace in her hands to her face. Betrayal distinctly flashed across his eyes, and she didn't miss the underlying hurt within their depths.

But before she managed to call after him, he turned on his heel and disappeared down the hallway.

Vivienne slumped into a chair, massaging the ache in her temples now that they were the only two in the room. "This was rather forward and rude of the duke, don't you think? To send the gifts *here*? To another man's home? Could he at least have waited until we returned to the palace?" She shook her head and glanced toward the frost accumulated on the window. In a murmuring tone, she said, "And to send a servant in *this* weather…"

Her mother nonchalantly fanned her face as the window drew her gaze to the snow flitting to the ground. "You are not courting the viscount, at least not officially. As far as the duke is concerned, he has no competition for your affection. He can very well do as he pleases."

"Mother—"

"Vivienne," she interrupted, lowering her voice as if to keep anyone from hearing their conversation from the hallway. "This might very well be our last day here. You must get Lord Beaumont to kiss you by the night's end."

"It's impossible."

"Ha!" She fanned her face faster. "You did it once within hours. You can do it again. Don't make me remind you how important this is."

"I know."

She hefted a sigh as she placed the jewels back into the box and left it on the table. Although she wanted nothing to do with being married to the duke, she also knew she couldn't throw away his offer of marriage when to do so could possibly destroy her family. She was fortunate to have such an offer. She knew that.

But it caused her heart to ache, nonetheless.

"Do you love him?" her mother asked quietly. They both knew she wasn't speaking of the duke.

"Love is not a factor after what I face."

"I loved and still love your father. I've always wanted you to find love for yourself as well. I've wanted it for you and all your siblings."

Vivienne crossed the room in several strides, stroking the short strand of hair beneath the rest where she had cut it to give to Edward weeks ago. Could he have disposed of it after all this time? "I have loved him my entire life. In different ways, of course, throughout the years. But I would think I would be heartbroken to lose him now."

"Then you mustn't give up."

Tears pooled in her eyes as she placed her hand over her belly. The task to make him fall in love with her, too, seemed impossible. But if she had one more day to catch his eye, then she wouldn't rest until she accomplished the feat.

Vivienne rubbed her gloved hands together for warmth. An anxious breath escaped her as a cloud of frost from where she stood at the base of Edward's tower. A dim light flickered from his window, but knowing he was up there caused nervous butterflies to flutter about in her stomach. She wasn't normally one to give into anxiety, but her entire future rested on one more adventure.

The snow had stopped, and judging by the gossip circulating the estate, most everyone predicted the majority would melt before tomorrow afternoon. One more day to woo Edward certainly was not enough time. A part of her feared his rejection should she fail.

The rock in her hand seemed to grow heavier the longer she stood staring up at the tower. The anxious part of her urged her to flee back into the house and let the matter drop. But another part of her recalled Edward's tears earlier that week.

Why was he upset? Had something happened? What was the root of his sadness?

Remembering the devastation in his eyes gave her the courage she needed to pull back her arm and throw the rock toward the window. It missed the glass and bounced off the brick instead.

But Edward seemed to hear it, as the window creaked open moments later.

"Edward!" she hissed in the darkness. "Let down your hair!"

Right on time, his head appeared over the sill with a scowl on his face. "Might I point out that *your* hair is marginally longer than *mine*?"

She only smiled at him, enjoying the way the dark strands fell over his face. His hair was chin-length at best. But she did so enjoy teasing him.

Plus, she found a moment to appreciate the silhouette of his build against the backdrop of the light from his room. He was handsome and had a body type she just adored—tall and long-limbed, but with enough muscle to make her feel safe and secure.

"Bundle up," she ordered. "You're coming down tonight."

"I..." Edward cleared his throat from above. "I can't tonight. I'm not...I'm not feeling well."

"Oh, pish posh. If you are scared of me, why don't you tell me outright?"

"I am not scared of you," he defended. "I cannot do this." He gestured between the two of them, though his meaning was lost on her. Was he speaking of their friendship? A romantic tryst? Sneaking out? Or was he truly not feeling well?

"You are going to have to be clearer," she sang, "and stop speaking in riddles."

He leaned against the window, and only then did she notice how pale he looked, almost as if he *had* been ill all day. "If we are caught, it will ruin your chances with the duke. I can't do that to you."

A long, frustrated sigh escaped her. Mostly frustration at her situation. She was not interested in the duke, but she could not dismiss him entirely because of self-preservation and the good reputation of her family.

But she also needed to reel Edward in, so she told him the truth. "Duke Hastings is unsuccessfully trying to woo me. Now get down here, or I will find a way to climb up there."

"Vivi..." Her name on his lips was almost pleading. Perhaps a warning.

"I have time." No, she didn't. "I want to find the right partner. Not the wrong one."

After a long moment, he ducked back inside and closed the window behind him. And then the light snuffed out from within.

Her heart fell at the sudden dismissal, falling out of her chest and splatting on the ground. The man was secretive, keeping things from her. Why couldn't he speak his mind? Tell her the truth? Confide in her?

Rather, he was dancing on eggshells, careful not to break them beneath his feet. But what if those eggshells were stronger than he realized?

Her pulse jumped when the window opened again, and the same sheets she'd climbed up the other night tumbled over the sill. Hurriedly, she picked up her heart and slammed it back into her chest as she watched him throw one leg over the side of the window, quickly followed by the other.

Suddenly, she realized how he might have felt watching her climb up as she watched him climb down. Her heart clung to her throat, terrified he might slip on the slick stone and fall and break a bone or two.

But when his feet landed on solid ground, she relaxed. Climbing towers was not an ideal way of sneaking around and spending time with someone she cared for, but she would do what she must to make this work.

Not giving him a chance to recover from the feat, she giggled as she took his hand, and the two of them raced away from the estate and closer to the forest bordering the property. Edward led her through an obscure path to prevent someone from spotting them, and soon, they raced into the cover of the trees and into the safety and solitude of the forest.

Edward slowed first, gasping and breathing heavily as if the short journey had exhausted him.

"Sitting behind a desk all day slowing you down?" She playfully pinched his side, and he responded with a weary smile. Somehow, he appeared even paler than before, truly struggling to breathe. "Edward?"

He held up a hand as if to say to give him a moment, and she made a mental note not to run again lest he collapse entirely. It was almost comical the way he no longer had the lungs he used to years ago, as if the desk truly had stripped him of physical exertion.

After a few moments, he lowered himself on a root jutting out from the ground and leaned back against the trunk of a large tree. The sight of the tall trees surrounding her, jutting roots, and low, overhanging branches brought back many memories of hours spent with her childhood friend. Oh, the adventures they'd had within these forests!

"Our secret place is much different now that we're adults, isn't it?" she asked, running her fingers over the damp bark of what used to be her tree. She'd climbed as high as she could one day just to glimpse the edge of the world.

"You simply need a bit of imagination." He gestured toward a group of pines, much larger than she remembered them. "Over here we have the ballroom. And this..." He motioned toward the tangled roots to his right. "It's the valley of fire and destruction."

"I remember!" she laughed, picking up her skirts and stepping over a few of the roots to reach into the nearby tree.

And then she gasped as she spotted a cluster of pinecones. "New treasures! Come look."

But he shook his head, still struggling for breath. "In a minute."

She tsked, wagging a finger at him. "The bedsheet rope is not the best idea. We need to think of something else."

"I used to have a trellis I was able to climb down."

"What happened to it?"

He shrugged sheepishly. "I got caught. Clara had it removed."

"How long ago was that?"

"Oh, I must have been sixteen or seventeen then." He snorted, shaking his head. "And then I managed to hide a ladder in the sky parlor above my room. I promptly got that taken away after I failed to return to it fast enough after..." He rubbed the back of his neck in a sheepish manner. "After the masquerade. A servant found it. And once again, I was caught."

The fact that he was locked in his room every night was concerning enough. Since he was at least sixteen? "Why are they doing this to you? You are the lord of the house. It doesn't seem right."

He pressed his lips together, visibly shrinking away from her and closing himself off. Like everyone else, he wouldn't speak of the reasoning behind such drastic actions. But if he didn't want to divulge the information, then she wouldn't press him. At this point, she knew she was missing some relevant information. He wasn't in legal trouble, which she had written off days earlier. A controlling sister, perhaps?

It seemed as if Clara controlled estate affairs, which only made sense when she was years older than him and had to take over when their parents had died. But then did that mean

Edward didn't have a backbone? Or was something else going on that she couldn't figure out on her own?

Finally, Edward pushed himself to his feet and joined her beside the tree. A soft smile reached his mouth as he picked up one of the pinecones and turned it around in his fingers. "We never did finish that game of treasure hunting, did we?"

"No, we certainly did not."

She watched as he stripped a small, wet, flexible branch from a tree, stringing on an eye-sized pinecone followed by another.

"Tell me the truth," she demanded playfully with a hand resting on her hip. He glanced up with an alarmed expression, at least until he seemed to notice her kittenish attitude. "You know who organized the masquerade, don't you?"

He returned her grin with one of his own. "If I tell you," he said, reaching across the space between them to place a finger against her lips, "I must swear you to secrecy."

Wordlessly, she nodded.

He dropped his hand. "My friends and I set it up every year. Tobie chose the location this time. It's one of Barnaby's vacant properties."

"And I never received an invitation?" She gave him a mock pout. "I had to resort to stealing one. I'm most disappointed."

"You were seventeen when the invitations were sent, apparently." He laughed, stringing on another few pinecones and tying a knot in the branch between each one. "Eighteen and older only. But no older than thirty-nine, and only if we deem one worthy of an invitation."

"Would I have received one?" She fluttered her eyelashes at him, and he grinned.

"And risk the warlord's hot iron against our throats? Not likely."

"Oh." Her spirits fell when, once again, her father's position threatened how she wanted to *live* and not just go along with life like a porcelain doll. The harsh restraints on her lifestyle were why she'd done reckless things in the past. Because she wanted the thrill of adventure.

And of course, that desire had gotten her into deep trouble.

"Turn around," Edward instructed softly.

Giving him a curious glance, she did as he asked, facing the other way. But then her heart picked up as she heard him approach, stopping directly behind her. His heat seeped into her back. His breath caressed her ear.

And then he draped the strand of pinecones over her neck, tying it in the back with a few tugs.

She blinked rapidly as emotion crashed into her, her fingers caressing the beautiful gift. She had received gorgeous, expensive jewels from the duke, but they paled in comparison to this simple offering. Because the gift was heartfelt, filled with friendship, promises, and dare she think it, love.

"Perhaps our treasure hunt is over now," he murmured near her ear. "Because we found the most exquisite jewels lying at the bottom of the sea."

"I love them."

Before he could see how her eyes pooled with emotion, she spun around, grabbed a fistful of his coat, and pulled him down for a kiss. Heat sparked between them. Stronger than ever when so much time had passed since their last kiss. The heat from his soft lips jumped into her body, filling her with the most pleasant warmth from the man she cared about most in the world.

But she was still scared, afraid to give him a chance to either kiss her back or reject her advances. Therefore, she broke the kiss all too quickly and ducked out of their secret spot while her laughter trailed behind her.

"Catch me if you can!" she called back to him.

She broke out of the treeline and faced a glittering lake reflecting the light of the moon off its rippling surface. It took a moment to locate the small boat resting upside down on the rocky shore, but when she found it, she brushed off the layer of snow gathered on it and tipped it over with great effort, relieved to find it in good condition after all these years.

Edward appeared out of the trees, his gait slow and his expression dazed. She'd clearly taken him off guard with the kiss. And the way his heated glance took her in... He'd undoubtedly felt something with their shared kiss. Would he want to try again?

But this time, she needed him to take the reins. She'd cast the line. Now would he bite?

"Don't get your shoes wet," he cautioned as they pushed the boat into the water until it scraped against the bottom of the lake. "Your toes will never forgive you."

She settled down on one of the two benches, allowing him to push them the rest of the way into the water before he hopped in after her. The boat rocked with the movement, and before he took the opposite seat, his hand brushed over his heart, his breathing labored at the simple action.

"Edward?" Worry leaked into her voice, as this wasn't the first time he'd struggled with a physical activity. "Are you up to rowing? I'm fully capable of handling it myself."

"Hmm?" he asked distractedly before his gaze landed on her. "No, I can do it."

He dipped both oars into the freezing but not quite iced-over lake, the boat cutting smoothly through the water while a serene stillness descended upon the night. Vivienne inhaled a deep breath, enjoying the way the fresh air created a pleasant chill in her lungs. High above them, the silver stars twinkled like gems on the dark canvas.

It was one of the most beautiful nights she'd ever experienced. But it likely had to do with the company she kept as well.

"It's beautiful," he murmured, echoing her thoughts out loud. "I enjoy looking at the stars. There is so much we don't know. So much I want to learn. There's not enough time…" He cleared his throat and tore his gaze away from the sky. "Not enough time to learn and observe like I wish to do."

"Your work must keep you busy. I can't imagine what responsibilities you must face every day."

The rhythmic splash of water as the oar dipped into the lake brought a measure of peace into her soul. Somehow, she knew everything would turn out all right. She didn't need to fear the future as much as she currently did. Things would work themselves out.

But she needed to help it along.

They rowed in silence for several minutes, each enjoying the stillness of the atmosphere, not needing to converse to fill the hush. She felt as if she could remain by his side, not a single word uttered between them, and still feel a measure of peace and comfort in his presence.

She glanced across the boat to find him staring intensely at the water, a frown puckered on the corners of his mouth.

His attention seemed far away, almost distracted. But she couldn't deny that she liked the way his mouth curved when in deep concentration, that she liked how a strand of black hair fell over his eye as he rowed. She enjoyed watching the movement of his arms as he rowed slowly, with unhurried movements. A cloud of breath escaped his lips, and despite the cold growing steadily chillier, he didn't complain once. Rather, it seemed as if he enjoyed the bitter sting just as she did.

What was he thinking about? Could he possibly be pondering a future with her? Or was she too hopeful?

Nervousness raced through her stomach as she tried to find a way to broach the topic of the future. Their close friendship had successfully returned after years of separation. But she needed something more. *Wanted* something more.

"Hmm," she said slowly, leaning back and gazing up at the stars to avoid looking at him. "You are twenty-three, no?"

"Mmhmm."

"Almost twenty-four."

A pause. "Yes."

Despite his obvious reluctance to want to speak about this, she barreled through while feigning ignorance of his discomfort. "I suppose Edilann law states you must be married by the time you turn twenty-four as a titled lord. Where are you hiding the women lining up at your door?"

But rather than earning a chuckle at her jest, he remained quiet.

She lowered her gaze to find him staring out over the dark waters of the lake, a troubled expression on his face. He'd stopped rowing, the boat now floating aimlessly in the middle of the body of water.

"I've never thought much about marriage," he finally answered. "It has always seemed like…like a distant dream I could never reach."

She furrowed her eyebrows. "Why? You are plenty handsome enough, if that's your worry."

This time, her words inspired a chuckle and a cheeky look. She much preferred seeing a smile on his face than a frown.

"There are no women lining up at my door." He shook his head and leaned an arm against the side of the vessel. "I have not been able to attend many outings, and therefore, I am simply a name rather than a face to most people in our circle."

Her face twisted into skepticism. "There are no women you are interested in, then? None at all?"

Oh, how she wanted to kick herself for sounding so…desperate. For being too involved. And perhaps a little too obvious. But tonight might very well be her last night to reel him in. And after her departure? Well, she wasn't sure how to woo him nor court him if he was an unwilling participant in society.

"It doesn't matter," he murmured before he closed off even further, shrinking back in his seat.

She tightened her fists in her lap, terror building up within her. Because she knew what she must do, what she must say. The *truth* she must speak. If he were to reject her, then he must do so knowing he was also rejecting their child.

"There is something I need to tell you." She braved lifting her head to meet his eye. "At the masquerade. When we… Well, when things went a little too far between us…"

"Forgive me," he interrupted, resting his elbows on his knees and leaning close enough for her to see the distress in his eyes. "I was not thinking clearly. I did not realize what damage I could do to your reputation. And when I learned who you really were, I was in a panic. I did not react as well as I should have, and for that, I am sorry."

"You were cold to me."

Edward released a long sigh and nodded. "I know."

"Did you not intend to find me?" A bubble of hysterics rose in her throat. Or perhaps it was bile, she wasn't sure. All she knew was she was nauseous and terrified and uncertain. "I searched for you for weeks, Edward. I attended every social gathering possible, but I was convinced you made empty promises and abandoned me, telling me lies and running away. You seemed interested in me then. What was it that changed your mind?"

"You think I abandoned you?" he argued back. "I was bedridden for two weeks after the masquerade. I've been…sick. And every time I tried to leave the house, Clara prevented me from going. Why do you think I organized the ball behind my sister's back?" He gestured to her. "It was to lure you in, because I didn't know how else to find you."

"And how well did that work out for you, Edward? Hmm? When you were disappointed to learn of the identity behind the mask?"

"Disappointed?" He threw his hands up in the air, losing control of his careful emotions. "My best friend I've ever had was behind that mask. Imagine my *horror* when I realized I might have ruined her life." His voice cracked, and her heart cracked along with it. "My only disappointment has been that you stopped visiting me after my parents died. I have other friends, but it's not the same as the connection I shared with you."

"My parents' reason for visiting was gone. What could I have done? I was just a child then."

"And so was I."

"Confound it, Edward! I love you!"

At the unexpected declaration from her mouth, he burst into tears, shaking his head as he covered his face with his hands. "You cannot love me. Do not do this. I beg you." He continued to sob, a distressing, heartbroken sound. "I beg you, Vivi."

Vivienne sat back in her seat, holding her hands tight against her heart as it began to shatter. But no matter how hard she tried to hold in the broken pieces, they slipped between her fingers and scattered to the bottom of the lake.

She had her answer.

And now she realized it was in her best interest to not tell him about the baby. No one could know the truth, not even him, when she must pretend the baby belonged to another man.

As tears trailed down her face and froze to her cheeks, she took the oars from him and began rowing them back toward shore. She never knew love could hurt so much. A part of her wished she'd never had the chance to find out.

They reached shore far too fast but not quickly enough. And when she stepped out of the boat, she didn't look back, not a single time, as she quickened her pace toward the estate.

She'd taken a chance. She'd given her all. But it wasn't enough.

Edward Beaumont did not love her.

And now her heart was broken beyond repair.

Chapter Ten

Packing was a dismal activity.

The maids insisted on helping, but Vivienne refused, needing something to occupy her hands, her attention, other than her broken heart.

She'd been reckless, and now she was paying the price. She would have a dreary husband twice her age, spending every waking moment as his wife while she loved another. It wasn't fair to the duke. It wasn't fair to herself.

But no other choice remained.

She carefully placed her blue gown into the portmanteau, thinking about how not even that could draw the viscount's attention. And with shaking hands, she untied the pinecone necklace from around her neck and set it on top.

It was time to say goodbye to her hopes and dreams and fancies. To the love in her heart. The duke would rule her with an iron thumb, restricting her adventures and curbing her playfulness.

Her chest ached as she recalled reading with Edward beneath the sheets in playful voices. Racing through the forest hand in hand. Laughing together until the break of dawn. She'd loved every moment spent with him, because their souls were one of the same. Meant for each other.

If only he could feel it, too.

A knock sounded on the door. She jumped and swiped a hand across her cheeks before composing herself and opening the door.

A maid curtsied on the opposite side, handing her a package wrapped in brown paper tied with a cream-colored ribbon. "For her ladyship."

Before Vivienne found the mind to inquire further, the maid disappeared and left her by her lonesome.

Closing the door behind her, she took a seat on the window bench, the chill from the glass seeping inside the room. She found nothing on the outside of the package to indicate its sender, and for one disappointing moment, she thought it might be another gift from the duke.

But as she pinched the ribbon and pulled, the paper fell away to reveal a large volume. Not just any book, but the very one Edward had read to her beneath the flickering lantern light days ago.

Her heart caught in her throat as she reverently stroked the weathered leather spine and ran a finger along the worn edges. Carefully, she opened the book to where the ribbon bookmark had been placed, giving a start when an envelope fell out of its pages.

A shudder of anticipation worked its way through her limbs as she broke the wax seal on the brown envelope, and then she slipped out a long page filled with messy script.

ADORINGLY, EDWARD

Dearest Vivienne,

All the glittering jewels could never surpass your beauty...

Ha! I'm jesting, though you are certainly a beautiful woman. I know I should not make such jests, but I simply couldn't pass up the opportunity.

She laughed, tears trailing from her eyes as she read Edward's words. He had always been able to coax a laugh out of her no matter the circumstance. Even during one of her darkest moments, he was still there, making her smile.

All jesting aside, I'm gifting you my most prized possession because now it's your turn to enjoy what stories are written within the pages. I've hoarded it for far too long now. Perhaps you will love it as much as I have. I should be most disappointed if every single page isn't hanging by a thread years from now.

Vivi, you must know that these past few months have been the best of my life. Thank you for making me feel alive, for giving me so much joy. I will treasure the days spent with you for the rest of my life.

Your Greatest Admirer,
Adoringly, Edward

Vivienne hugged the book to her chest, feeling each and every one of his words like a warm embrace. Perhaps not all was lost after all.

But even as hope blossomed within her, she quickly squashed it as she recalled last night and the way he had rejected her love. There was no hope for them.

She just didn't quite know how to accept it.

"Everything will be all right, little one," she murmured as she rubbed her belly. If only she believed the words herself.

Her mother strode into the room at that moment, pausing as her attention lingered on her belly. Quickly, Vivienne dropped her hand, her cheeks flaming as she stared at the ground.

"No more of that until you are married." She gestured to all of her with her fan. "Duke Hastings is to call on us at the palace in two days' time. Should he propose, I expect you to accept."

Holding back the emotions threatening to capsize her, she nodded dutifully. To protect her family from her mistakes, she would do what she must.

"Then let us depart. We've been away from home long enough."

But as they climbed in their carriage and left the estate, Vivienne couldn't help thinking as the property grew smaller and smaller from the window…

She was leaving the only place that had truly felt like home.

And she may never see it nor the man who held her heart again.

"How is he doing?" a voice asked from outside his bedroom door.

Edward's attention shifted blearily from the book in his lap and toward the door closed between himself and whomever resided in the stairwell. He could hardly read the words, anyway, when they kept blurring, making reading difficult.

"Not well," Clara answered quietly as if the two of them didn't think he could hear them.

He turned his head toward Cedric, who sat in a nearby chair reading his own book, which rested atop a bouncing knee. "Who's here?"

"I believe your uncle had planned to visit today," his servant replied quietly.

Although Edward's attention returned to the door, he couldn't bring himself to stand. He couldn't even lift his head from where it rested against the back of his chair. The outing with Vivienne had taken an enormous toll on his body.

A frown pulled on his mouth, his heart aching as he recalled her tears, the way she'd fled, and how he hadn't been able to find the strength to climb back up his tower. He'd stumbled into the servants' quarters to find Cedric, and he'd helped him climb the set of stairs leading to his room.

Of course, Cedric had taken the bedsheet rope away from him to "wash it," but he knew he wasn't going to see it again in his lifetime.

It was just as well. He wouldn't be seeing Vivienne again, either.

His hand moved to his breast pocket where her lock of hair resided within a folded handkerchief. He needed to let her go.

He just didn't know how.

Finally, he recognized Uncle Maxwell's voice. "What can we do?" he asked in a distressed tone. "Should we try a new medicine? We can't lose him, Clara."

"We've tried everything possible. What more can we do?"

After a few moments of silence, someone knocked on the door. When his voice refused to cooperate when he tried to call out for them to enter, Cedric stepped in for him.

"Come."

Uncle Maxwell entered the room with Clara at his heels, a worried look in her eyes. Maxwell adopted a cheery expression as if wanting to believe Edward would make it through this.

But they all knew he wouldn't.

Cedric abandoned his chair and made himself scarce on the opposite side of the room while his uncle replaced him. It created a physical ache in Edward's chest at just how alike his uncle and late father looked to one another. Similar black hair. The same hazel eyes. They'd had such a good friendship between brothers, and Edward had looked up to him all his life because of it.

"How are you faring today?" his uncle asked as if he had not just asked his sister the same question a minute earlier.

"As well as I can be."

The other man leaned forward on his knees and smiled reassuringly. "I've been in contact with a physician from across the sea. He can be here in a month from now. Many of his methods are more extreme. But they are tried and proven, and I'm hoping they can help."

"I'm not sure if he would arrive soon enough."

"It's worth a try."

Edward didn't refute him nor agree with him. Short of performing a heart surgery no one thought was possible, one that would more likely kill him than allow him to live, nothing would help.

"Let's play a game." Maxwell crossed the room and opened the cupboard filled with games and books, pulling out one of

Edward's favorites. But then he paused before picking up Vivienne's blue and white lacy fan he'd forgotten to give back to her all this time.

"Put that down."

But instead, his uncle unfurled it, laughing as he fanned his face. He read the initials carved into the wood. "'V.W.' I think my little nephew has a paramour."

"I said put it down."

Finally, his uncle held up his hands as if to show he meant no harm before setting it back where it belonged. "For both of your sakes, I hope the new doctor arrives sooner rather than later."

Uncle Maxwell sat down, forgetting to close the cupboard behind him. For a long few moments, Edward stared at Vivienne's fan resting on top of one of his books. For the remainder of his life, he would treasure the time he'd had with her, however short, keeping the memory of her locked within his weak heart.

He loved her.

And he hadn't realized just how much until she was gone.

"He can't bother to come see me himself?" Vivienne scoffed as she set down a bottle of imported perfume on the table in the family suite. It smelled awful. Like heartbreak and defeat.

"Duke Hastings is visiting tomorrow," her mother reminded her.

"If he really were competing for my hand, he would show up at my door like a thoughtful gentleman."

Her sister, Sophia, raised an eyebrow from where she sat beside the hearth while embroidering flowers on the bodice of one of her dresses. "Competing with whom?"

Another sister, Marcella, elbowed the other in the ribs. "Don't be rude. She captured the duke's attention. She needs no other serious suitors."

The look her mother gave warned her not to speak of Edward. But rather than finding gratitude deep within herself for the duke's special attention, she only uncovered anger. Anger at her stupidity, at her selfishness, at losing her freedom and the man she loved.

By tomorrow, she needed to come to terms with becoming the wife of a duke. But today?

She preferred to feel red, hot anger.

Without another glance at the vast amounts of gifts atop the table, she strode out of the room, stomped down the staircase, and snatched her cloak from a waiting servant before slumping onto a bench in the entryway, sitting by her lonesome while glaring at the wall on the opposite side of the room.

Anger was unbecoming of a woman of good breeding, her mother had told her countless times. But Vivienne felt things too deeply. It was no easy task to hide the rage and devastation billowing inside of her.

"Thank you very much," a voice said, floating down the nearby hallway and reaching her ears. "I will send for the documents next week."

The earl, Lord Barnaby Mavis, also one of Edward's close friends, appeared around the corner with a coat draped over one arm. He paused in his tracks the moment he caught her eye.

"Lady Vivienne," he greeted as he brushed his blond hair out of his face. But a hesitancy rested in his vivid blue eyes, a quiet word lurking behind his tongue.

"Lord Mavis." She pulled off her slippers and reached for her boots. A bit of fresh air to sting her cheeks was exactly what she hoped would calm the fire in her spirit.

But the man continued to stand in the middle of the room, clearly wanting to say something.

"How was your stay at the Beaumont residence?" he finally asked, taking another step closer.

"Splendid," she replied sarcastically. "Just peachy."

"Edward was that bad, huh? He's usually a good host."

"Usually?" she scoffed. "Well, I'm sure you've seen him more recently than I have." She angrily clasped her cloak around her shoulders. "He hadn't even the decency to say goodbye." She furiously shoved her feet into her boots. "He'll turn twenty-four soon and find the wife he's always wanted, and then live happily ever after like in his storybooks."

Barnaby turned dangerously quiet, and she lifted her head to find him covering his mouth with his hand. "You don't know."

"Don't know what?"

He lowered himself on a chair near her so they were eye level. But his characteristic smile had long since disappeared in favor of a devastated frown. "The doctor gave Edward less than three months more to live. He likely won't survive long enough to see his twenty-fourth birthday."

"Pardon?" she breathed, reaching out to the wall to steady herself when his words rushed over her head, too quickly for her to make sense of. "You must be mistaken. He's in the prime of his health."

But then she recalled all the times Edward had been gasping for breath after physical exercise, struggling with even the simplest of tasks.

"He's had a severe heart condition all his life. He keeps it a secret, as it threatens his title and position as viscount should others learn of it. Only his closest family and friends know of it." He ran a hand through his golden locks. "It's only gotten worse in the last year."

Shock washed over her, filling her blood with a numbing cold. "He told me he was sick for two weeks after the masquerade."

Barnaby nodded. "His heart can only handle so much. It's why Clara locks him in the tower. Someone needs to know where he is at all times. It keeps him safe, as much as he hates it. The episodes can be dangerous if he's alone without help."

Vivienne scrubbed a hand down her face as the information finally sank in enough for the breath to flee her lungs entirely. "They locked him in his room as he slept for three days when I was there."

"Like I said, his condition is worsening. I think it was his body's way of trying to recuperate—by shutting down for a few days."

She buried her face in her hands as she tried to recall every conversation, every interaction with him. Was this why he wouldn't entertain a relationship between them? Because he knew he was going to die?

"Why would he keep this from me? I bore my heart and soul to him and he rejected me."

She felt silly revealing this to a near-stranger, as she and Barnaby were acquaintances at best. But he understood the situation. He was all she had.

A soft chuckle escaped him, but the amusement didn't reach his eyes. "He went to great lengths to figure out who you were, his masquerading dame. I assure you that if he felt confident that he could pursue you, he would."

"He does not care for me."

He shook his head. "No, Vivienne. He cares so much that he's letting you go. What more can he do? He's dying."

Her numbing shock slowly melted until paralyzing fear overcame her. All this time, Edward had been dying?

Now she truly understood why he had wanted to escape by attending the masquerade. Now she truly understood why he'd snuck out and allowed her to sneak in. He wanted to live life before he couldn't anymore.

Each heartbeat pounded painfully slow as she imagined life without Edward in it. Oh, how he must have been suffering! To keep this from her while pasting a smile on his face.

"I thought he was avoiding me because..." She didn't finish her sentence. She didn't know *how*. Although it had been a stupid choice to make love to Edward, she could never regret it.

"I am denying any knowledge of the events of the masquerade." He inspected his nails. "I know nothing."

Oh, but he certainly *did* know. She narrowed her eyes at him. "Who else has Edward told?" she said in a hissing whisper.

"Ah, well, a few of us know. But we'd die before revealing his secret. I promise you."

Devastation filled her at the thought of losing Edward, especially to sickness. She could not marry the duke knowing Edward might be giving her up because he wasn't going to last much longer in this life.

She could not do it. Not anymore.

"What do I do, Barnaby?" she asked miserably, scrubbing her hands down her face. She felt lost and confused and terrified for so many different reasons.

"Do about what?" He raised an eyebrow, clearly not understanding.

Lowering her voice, she couldn't help the tremor in her words as she placed a hand over her belly to silently convey her meaning. "What do I do?"

"Dear heavens." Barnaby ran a hand through his hair, glancing back and forth across the entry room as if to make sure they were alone. "Vivienne, this is serious."

"I know," she replied despairingly. "I have been trying to attract Edward's attention, to get him to propose at least somewhat willingly. But I'm running out of time. And it seems he is, too."

A sinking pit in her stomach grew increasingly larger at the reminder.

"He doesn't know."

She shook her head. "I'm too scared he will abandon us."

Barnaby patted her hand, offering her solace when the darkness of confusion and heartache swirled around her. "He cannot help you if he doesn't know. He will not abandon you. I promise you this."

When she likely didn't appear convinced, he patted her hand again and gave her fingers a reassuring squeeze. "*I* will help you, Vivienne. That is the first step. And the next will be Edward."

"Thank you," she sobbed, her hand flying to her mouth. Suddenly, she didn't feel quite so alone. Her mother had told her to tell no one, to trust no one. But she felt safe telling

Edward's friend of her situation. He wouldn't abandon her. And she must believe Edward wouldn't, either.

"Now..." he said as he handed her a handkerchief from his pocket to dab her eyes. "Here's what we will do."

Chapter Eleven

"Wake up."

Edward slowly pulled himself out of the daze of sleep as someone shook his shoulder. His groggy mind tried to make sense of his spinning surroundings and the voice flitting barely out of reach. For the life of him, he couldn't lift his head from his pillow, and no amount of distraction could erase the aches and pains traveling through every corner of his body.

"It's time to go," the person said again, and finally, Edward's unfocused gaze landed on a familiar head of blond hair, a pair of blue eyes staring down at him.

"Barnaby," he croaked. "What hour is it?"

"Mid-morning," he answered before crossing the length of his room and throwing open his clothing chest. One at a time, he pulled articles of clothing from within and tossed them onto the foot of the bed. "You can't live like this. I don't care how exhausted you are. You have to get out of bed."

"I can't."

He squeezed his eyes shut to block out the ceiling spinning above him.

But then Barnaby threw a coat over his head.

As much as he wanted to brush it aside, his arms refused to move.

His friend's head appeared moments later as he pulled the garment down. "You must really be tired."

All he managed was a long exhale.

Cedric approached the bed, and on the count of three, they hefted Edward into a sitting position, dressed him despite his mumbled protests, and hoisted him to his feet. A sudden agony smashed into his skull and worked its way into his chest. Dying had never felt so awful.

When his voice refused to work, he held out a shaky hand, and Cedric placed an unstopped medicine vial within his fingers. Some of the liquid slopped onto the front of his coat, but he managed to get it mostly down his throat, cringing at the bitter taste.

The medicine helped with the pain while also making him sleepy. He wanted to disappear as far into the recesses of his mind as his body would allow, if only to escape a fraction of the agony.

With a friend on either side of him, they helped him descend the staircase one step at a time, each movement painful and tiring.

And when they entered the foyer of the estate...

Both Clara and Maxwell watched him with pinched expressions, their distress a mirror of the other. And little James... The boy watched him with tear-filled eyes. If only Edward could give him some reassurance that he wasn't going anywhere.

"He should not be leaving home," Clara protested. "Look at him! He can hardly stand on his own."

"Oh, Clara," Barnaby tsked, and Edward immediately caught onto the layers of charm he smoothed out of his mouth. "You have been doing such a wonderful job looking after him. You need a break. I'll return him safe and sound after our outing."

"And where, exactly, are you going?" Maxwell asked, arms crossed over his chest.

"To my home. His friends need to spend at least one last day with him before the snow falls in earnest."

Still, Maxwell continued to frown, his worried gaze sweeping over him. "Have him back before dusk. Cedric goes with him."

After agreeing to his uncle's terms, they helped him outside. A chilly wind rushed over him, far too unpleasant when his throat cried out in protest. But he pushed through the cold and allowed the others to help him into Barnaby's waiting carriage.

"Where are we *really* going?" Edward croaked out as he leaned his head against the back of the seat and gratefully accepted the blanket his friend draped over his lap.

"To make a quick stop at the palace. Or not so quick. I haven't decided yet."

"That's the last place I want to go."

"Then it's the first place we need to stop."

Why, oh why, is this the man I will have to accept? Vivienne lamented, pasting a smile on her face as Duke Hastings' long-winded monologue about his dedication to the Mother Goddess transitioned into another detailed explanation about why horses were measured in hands.

She had no qualms about her future husband being rather religious. She also possessed no misgivings about all the interesting facts spouting from the man's mouth.

But what she immensely disliked was not taking a breath in his lengthy speech to give her a chance to reply. The man cared nothing about her opinions nor about what she might like to say.

The moment the duke paused to take a sip of his tea, Vivienne cut into the one-sided conversation, "Duke, let me tell you about—"

"—and the horse was a beautiful breed, imported overseas from the finest breeder in all the world."

Across from her, Sophia's eyes widened as if sitting through the visit was complete torture, and she mouthed, *By the stars, won't he ever shut up?*

Marcella feigned stabbing her ears with an invisible object, clearly growing impatient herself.

Vivienne laughed at her sisters but disguised it as a cough as she covered up the sound with her hand. Their mother glared.

Duke Hastings was unfortunately confident that everyone around him was interested in hanging onto his every word. His conversational skills were weak at best, and she despairingly knew that as his wife, she would get pushed to the background and ignored, only to do her duty to bear an heir.

A smug part of her took heart in knowing the first child would not be his. She hoped the baby came out with hair as black as midnight just to spite him.

Internally, she chastised herself for such unkind thoughts. Duke Hastings was not a bad man. She would be lucky to become a duchess.

If only it was what she actually wanted…

But she pushed the heartbreaking thoughts away and replaced it with another tight smile as the duke changed the subject yet again to drone on about a business trade he'd conducted with another kingdom.

Her eyelids were on the verge of drooping with boredom when a knock sounded on the door, and a servant announced another arrival. "Lord Barnaby Mavis."

She immediately straightened, her gaze darting toward the door.

Moments later, Barnaby entered, giving a polite bow to each of them. Never in her life had she been so relieved for an interruption during a social visit, especially knowing that he might have brought Edward with him.

But as she craned her neck to glance into the hallway, she found it empty.

Her heart fell when she realized Edward hadn't arrived with him.

"Forgive my intrusion," he said, giving her mother and sisters a winning smile, enough for Marcella to snap open her fan and cool her heated face. When the man had married earlier that year, he'd broken many hearts, including her sisters'. "My wife, Ivette, is in the most dire straights, and has requested I steal Lady Vivienne for a few moments."

"Right now?" her mother asked, clearly not pleased with the change of events. But when Barnaby flashed her another smile, the woman actually giggled and dismissed Vivienne with a wave of her hand. "Fine enough." And then she turned to the duke. "You will forgive us for cutting this meeting short. Perhaps there is something you'd like to ask my daughter?"

No! Please, no. I'm not ready.

Nothing could ever prepare her for getting shackled to the duke. Therefore, she stood and curtsied, trying to slowly escape across the room. But then she tried not to grimace as he caught onto her hand and gave her fingers a kiss.

"May I call on you tomorrow morning?" he asked quietly. The intent in his eyes was unmistakable. Tomorrow, he planned to propose. Well, it was better than today. It at least gave her one more day to prepare for the inevitable.

Dread climbed her throat and turned to bile. It was all she could do to dip her head in what she hoped was an amicable nod. Once she was engaged to the duke, there was no turning back.

He deserves better than to be lied to, she thought to herself, guilt rising in her chest as she curtsied one last time and followed Barnaby out of the room. Although she didn't like the duke, he wasn't a bad man.

Barnaby stopped at the top of the staircase, and she glanced over the landing in search of a head of black hair. Disappointment rained over her when she only spotted servants quietly going about their tasks for the day.

"He won't come in," Barnaby said as if reading her thoughts.

"Why?" she despaired. "Does he dislike the idea of being anywhere near me so much?"

His lips thinned, and he shook his head, glancing around them before speaking quietly. "He cannot get out of the carriage. His body is too exhausted."

"Oh, poor Edward. I did not realize the extent of his ailment."

"He hides it well."

They said nothing more as they descended the staircase, bundled up in their cloaks, and exited the estate. Her heart pounded an anxious drum in her chest when she spotted Barnaby's waiting carriage. She didn't know what to expect from their meeting. All she knew was it was time they were honest with one another.

For the first time in weeks, Edward was too exhausted to move a single muscle in his body. He rested his head against the cool wall of the carriage and closed his eyes, knowing with a certainty that the doctor was wrong.

He wouldn't die in another few months.

He would be lucky if he made it another few weeks.

A choked exhale escaped his heavy lungs, the simple action of drawing a breath proving too difficult to muster. His limbs felt like lead. His head seemed too heavy to lift. Joining Barnaby on an outing had been a mistake. He'd prefer lying down for a spell to sitting upright in this miserable carriage.

The door of the carriage opened. Light spilled inside. And his momentarily relief transitioned into numbing shock when Vivienne peeked inside, a large smile spread across her face.

"Good morning!" she said cheerily, almost as if he hadn't broken her heart days earlier.

He shot upright, his eyes snapping wide open as his body suddenly found an elusive reserve of energy. "Vivi," he gasped.

Behind her, Barnaby helped her into the carriage and closed the door until only his face showed. He pointed to each of them in tandem. "You two are keeping monumental secrets from one another. You will not leave this carriage until both secrets are revealed." A pause. "Good luck."

And then he closed the door behind him.

Across from him, Vivienne let out a frosty breath as she took off her gloves and set them in her lap. "Well then," she continued cheerfully. "Why don't we start with your secret?"

Edward bit his lip, trapping his hands between his knees. The last thing he wanted was to witness her pitying gaze. He'd wanted to die with at least a small shred of dignity, to be remembered in her mind as strong and healthy.

"I'm sick," he finally said as he lifted his gaze. By the lack of surprise in her expression, he guessed Barnaby had already spilled his secret. "I'm *dying*. I should have told you ages ago. It's why..." He took a deep breath and let it out slowly when his heart began to act up, beating too quickly and making breathing difficult. "It's why I pushed you away. I cannot bear to hurt you. And growing too close to you will inevitably hurt you in the end. It's in your best interest to maintain your distance."

Her bottom lip turned downward in a strangely alluring frown. "Oh, Edward. It hurts me to know you have suffered so much. I wish you had not felt the need to distance yourself from me. I would have taken every minute you would have given me."

"That's not fair to you."

"It's not fair to me that you have been pushing me away. You know just how much I care about you, how much I value your presence and your conversation and your friendship. I am now beating myself up knowing I unknowingly put you at risk by forcing you to leave your tower."

"You never forced me."

She chuckled, shaking her head. "All right, *heavily persuaded*."

Still, dragging her down into the murky depths of his condition didn't sit well with him. "I still should have—"

"Eight weeks," she murmured, interrupting him long enough to pull his hands out from between his knees and press them to her heart.

He suddenly found himself at a loss for words when she stroked the back of his hands and kissed his palm. "What is eight weeks?"

A shuddering breath escaped her lips as she lifted her gaze. Fear flashed through her eyes. Her face paled. "It's been eight weeks since we were reunited. Eight weeks since we loved without abandon." A pause, followed by another shaky breath. "Eight weeks that I have been carrying your child."

Edward reeled back, every pore in his body icing over as his brain tried to make sense of her words. His arms fell limp when the shock made controlling his limbs difficult, but she never ceased holding onto his hands.

He stared back at her, searching in vain for a trace of laughter or a twitch of her mouth to indicate she might be teasing him. But he found nothing except seriousness and excessive worry.

"Tell me it's not true," he stammered. "Tell me you are jesting."

But when she shook her head, he slumped back in his seat, still reeling from the unexpected confession.

"I'm scared, Edward," she whispered when a reply flitted out of his reach. "My entire family will be ruined if anyone learns of it. That's why my mother feigned illness, to stay at your home and give me a chance to woo you. But you didn't want to be wooed."

He pulled away from her and buried his face in his hands. What terrible timing. Of course, he never should have taken liberties with her in the first place. But what was done was done. What was he supposed to do? He was dying, and because of it, he was ruining her life.

"Eight weeks," he murmured finally, meeting her gaze within the chilly carriage. "The baby would be born nearly two months earlier than expected should you marry *today*."

She blinked rapidly as if trying to keep tears from falling. "Why do you think I've been in a panic to find you?"

He groaned, rubbing a hand over his chest as his heart flipped and flopped inside him. "I didn't know, Vivi. I didn't know. You should have told me immediately."

"Immediately?" Her hysterics rose exponentially as she blinked more rapidly than before. "You *rejected* me immediately when I asked you to seek me out for a dance."

"What was I supposed to do?" he argued back. "My heart was too weak for dancing that day."

"And you couldn't have found another way to treat me rather than acting cold toward me? How hard would it have been to sit and talk?"

"I was in shock. I wasn't thinking clearly."

"No, no, no." She swiped at her eyes with the back of her hand. "All this time, I have been fighting for *you*. And all you have been doing is pushing me away."

"That's unfair. Considering my lack of knowledge about your predicament, I was pushing you away to save you from a life with a man on his deathbed!"

It was the wrong thing to say, because the moment the words left his mouth, Vivienne burst into tears, sobs escaping her mouth. Rather than arguing back, she threw open the door of the carriage and disappeared.

Somehow, Edward gathered the strength he needed to pursue her. His head spun as he stumbled down the single step of the carriage. He ignored Barnaby's grimace indicating he heard most, if not all, of their conversation. He ignored Cedric reaching out as if to steady him and chased after the woman he cared for most in this world.

The flap of green fabric drew his attention toward the entrance of the garden. He quickened his pace, his breaths coming too quick and his heart beating too fast. But they needed to have this conversation. Even if he had to crawl across hot coals to do it.

The moment she entered through green hedges, he grabbed onto her wrist to stop her from fleeing any farther.

"Answer me honestly," he begged, gasping for air. "Is this why you have been dallying with the duke? To spite me? Or for your own protection?" He squeezed his eyes shut for a moment when the world spun, and opened them to find that his vision refused to cooperate when he couldn't keep his gaze steady. "You said he was unsuccessful at wooing you. Did you lie?"

"What other choice do I have?" she cried, wrenching her arm away from him and throwing her hands into the air. "I cannot reject him because what else can I do?"

Despite her anger and hurt toward him, he reached for her again, this time holding her hands more gently to try to convey his sincerity. Because he needed—*wanted*—to make this right. "Marry *me*. It will protect your reputation, and you will be provided for after I die."

"Stop saying that," she choked. "You cannot die. I won't let you."

His ears started ringing. A blackness attacked the edges of his vision like angry bees.

No! he shouted at himself, gripping tighter onto her hands to keep him grounded in the present. He could not have an episode now. This conversation was too important.

But even as he fought against it, his heart lost control within his chest. His pulse thrummed quickly through his veins. The darkness in his eyes gathered as thick, relentless clouds.

"I've always wanted," he slurred, tipping precariously when he couldn't seem to keep his feet beneath him. "I've always wanted..."

He dropped one of her hands to clutch his chest. He gasped in another breath, stumbling to the side as he tried to keep himself on his feet.

He heard shouting in the distance. Words escaped Vivienne's mouth, her eyes wide with horror, but he couldn't make out the sound when the ringing drowned his ears.

"Marry me," he said again, pushing through his desperate proposal.

But then his body hit the ground with a thud, and the darkness overtook him.

Chapter Twelve

"EDWARD!" VIVIENNE SCREAMED, kneeling at his side after he collapsed.

She lifted his head into her lap, her fingers fluttering uselessly over him as he struggled to breathe, each breath quick and seemingly painful when his expression contorted with agony.

Moments later, Barnaby and Edward's personal servant, Cedric, dropped beside her. Cedric lifted Edward at the waist, propping his arms in the air as if to expand his lung capacity. Edward's head drooped to the side, each of his limbs limp.

"He's never been unconscious for one of these," Cedric grunted, sharing a worried look with Barnaby. But then he turned his attention toward her. "He needs a doctor. Is there one at the palace?"

"Yes!" she gasped, launching to her feet as terror for Edward nipped at her heels. "Get him inside one of the infirmary rooms. I'll fetch the physician."

She sprinted away, ignoring the alarmed looks she received from servants and other members of the court. Each footstep pounded a frantic rhythm across carpeted hallways and stone corridors until she burst into the infirmary.

Doctor Clark startled upright from his desk, a paper stuck to his face as he blinked the sleep from his eyes. He swiped the paper away and stood, his attention honing in on her. "Lady Vivienne."

He dipped into a bow.

"Do you have available rooms?" she gasped. "Lord Beaumont has collapsed."

The man's eyes hardened like a doctor with years upon years of experience dealing with patients. He gestured for her to follow him into a room with a small window lighting up a bed within a tight space and a table next to it. He grabbed several medical items and set them atop the table just as Cedric and Barnaby entered the room carrying unconscious Edward.

Her hand flew to her mouth as they laid him on the cot, still struggling to breathe. She clutched her hands to her chest as she stood in the corner, watching as the doctor barked out orders to the nurses. He spouted terms such as scalpel, thoracic drainage, and medications.

The doctor spoke to Barnaby, likely because he was a titled man who seemed to have his head on the straightest in that room. "If he doesn't respond to this medication, I will have to perform emergency surgery."

With help from the other men, they lifted Edward into a sitting position and forced a vial of liquid down his throat. Edward coughed and spluttered, wheezed and choked. Most of the medication splattered over his shirt, but whatever he *did* consume seemed to help calm his frantic lungs enough for them to try again with a second vial.

Thankfully, he responded to the medication, his breathing easing and his body slumping exhaustedly against the stack of pillows on the cot.

Vivienne cupped her face inside steepled fingers, thankful that Edward was recovering from the frightening ordeal.

"What happened?" she asked in a small voice, never once taking her attention off the man she loved.

"I believe one of his lungs collapsed," Doctor Clark answered. "Though, I can't figure out for the life of me why." He lifted his head and addressed Barnaby. "I know nothing of this patient. Tell me more of his medical history."

But Cedric answered, telling him of his severe heart condition and the symptoms associated with it. She found it difficult to hear just how much Edward had struggled with this for so many years, especially in the past year alone.

"Has he tried any remedies for his condition?" the doctor asked.

"Many. There is only one that has seemed to help, but I don't believe it works anymore other than to help him sleep."

"Where can I acquire a sample?"

Cedric reached into his breast pocket and produced a vial filled with translucent yellow liquid, handing it to the doctor. The man carefully inspected its contents, even pouring a small portion onto a piece of glass to view it closer. When he smelled it, his eyes hardened once again, He sniffed the contents several times, only managing to draw out the tension in the room when he said nothing for the longest time.

"What do you smell, Your Lordship?" Doctor Clark held out the vial.

Barnaby took it from him and swirled the liquid before bringing it to his nose. "It smells...acidic. A little bitter. And perhaps a hint of garlic."

Doctor Clark nodded. "Garlic is used in many herbal remedies. But I also caught the faint whiff of almond." Vivienne didn't know how the man's eyes could have possibly hardened any further, but somehow, he managed it as he crossed the room and closed the door between them and the nurses waiting outside.

"Doctor?" she asked. Unable to stay away from Edward for any longer, she pulled up a chair on the opposite side of the bed and rested her hand over his wrist.

"From how it sounds, Lord Beaumont's illness has worsened in the past year alone, while it has remained somewhat consistent in the years prior." He held up the vial again and frowned. "Arsenic poisoning produces many of the same effects as his heart condition. I reckon it would be easy to hide the symptoms behind his other symptoms."

Her jaw hung agape as she stared at the doctor, not believing her ears. "You believe he's been poisoned?"

"That is my guess, yes. A slow poisoning to make it unnoticeable."

She closed her eyes, a hand over her mouth. "Who would do such a thing?"

When she opened her eyes again, she found the two other men turning their heads in Cedric's direction.

The servant held up his hands in a show of peace. "I would never."

"We're not blaming you," Barnaby said in a frustrated growl, kicking the edge of the table. "You are one of the only people with access to the poisoned elixirs. Who else has access?"

"I don't know." Cedric ran a hand down his face. "Clara does. She often administers them herself. She gives them to me to give to Lord Beaumont."

"And..." The physician leaned forward in his chair with his elbows resting on his knees. "Has his current doctor not picked up on the change of ingredients?"

Vivienne gasped. "You're not saying his doctor..."

The man pressed his lips together. "I'm not casting blame at anyone. We're only finding ourselves a list of suspects."

"I told you," Cedric protested, "I would never harm him. He's my friend. I never questioned him once when he skipped his last few doses. Wouldn't you think I'd be more insistent if I were to blame?"

"When was his last dose?"

"This morning," Barnaby answered this time, running a hand along his jaw. "He wanted it to help make him sleepy because he was in a lot of pain."

Oh, my dear Edward.

The doctor nodded gravely. "To be unnoticeable, the dosages would have to be increased in small increments. If his body has been accustomed to higher and higher amounts of arsenic, consuming it again after a short break would have more dire consequences." He gestured to Edward's unconscious form. "This accounts for his most recent episode, more severe than the others."

She clasped her fingers together, praying to the Mother Goddess. "Will he live?"

"It's...hard to say right now. His lung needs to heal, and I hope it will be able to heal on its own with a bit of rest. We'll take one day at a time. Keep him out of his home until we find out who is responsible for the poisoning."

Finally, the man opened the door. "My staff will take good care of him. No one will enter the room without my permission. No one will administer anything to him without my permission." He looked at her as he reassured, "He is safe here. But he needs rest and medical care. Everyone needs to leave. Especially you, Your Ladyship. It isn't appropriate—"

Vivienne shot to her feet and interrupted him. "I'm his fiancée!" she cried, only wishing she had a ring to show a commitment to him. "He proposed right before his episode, and I have accepted. I will not leave his side."

Doctor Clark frowned, appearing unconvinced.

"It's true," Barnaby said, backing up her claim whether or not he actually believed it to be true. "I was witness to it. Let her stay with him."

"Very well. It would do him good to have a loved one by his side while we rid his body of the toxins."

One at a time, everyone filed out of the door, but Barnaby stopped in the doorway, glancing back at her and lowering his voice. "We need to find out who did this. I will involve the authorities, and I hope to investigate the matter quietly to prevent the one responsible from covering their tracks before we find them."

"What can I do?"

He smiled, though it didn't cover the worry in his eyes. "Keep him alive. I know firsthand how a beautiful lady can keep a man's heart pumping on his deathbed."

She stared at his retreating back, recalling the gossip she'd heard around the castle. Barnaby's horse had thrown him off a cliff and he'd hit his head, losing his memories at the time.

Ivette, his now wife, had nursed him back to health and helped him recover his memories.

Two nurses entered the room and tended to Edward. Taking his vitals. Checking his breathing. Ensuring his comfort even in unconsciousness. Vivienne continuously held his limp hand, keeping a finger over his disjointed pulse to reassure herself he still lived.

And when what seemed like hours later that Edward stabilized enough for nurses to check in periodically rather than constantly, Vivienne finally released a long, slow breath filled with relief. The doctor had reassured her that if he stabilized and didn't worsen, he had a high chance of surviving the attempted murder.

Finding herself alone with him for a few minutes, she braved the action of stroking his dark hair down to his stubbled cheek. She caressed his skin over the coarse texture, admiring how handsome he looked with a bit of scruff, as she'd only ever seen him clean shaven.

The dim light of a cloudy afternoon fell on his pale face, illuminating the way his chest rose up and down, uneven as if one of his lungs could only take in so much air compared to the other.

She scooted her chair closer and took his cold, limp hand in hers, pressing a tender kiss to his palm. "Don't you dare leave me, Edward. Stay for me. For us." She rested her other hand over her belly, hoping with all her might that they could one day be a family.

But he remained silent, his eyes closed and his chest rising and falling with each disjointed breath.

She recalled his episode and the terror of watching it unfold. It had been an extreme case. She knew that. But to watch helplessly as someone she loved suffered? Should Edward survive the attempt on his life, she would subject herself to watching him suffer for the rest of her life.

The thought created a pit of heartache within her, but she would stay by his side always. And she would suffer with him. Because she loved him.

And if he doesn't love you? an anxious voice whispered in her mind.

Vivienne swallowed the accompanying grief of unrequited love. He'd had several opportunities to confess if he returned her feelings. But he'd only proposed out of obligation. Not love.

"What is it?" she asked, frowning. "Am I too young for you? Am I too much like a friend? Are you interested in someone else?"

To distract her distressing thoughts, she eased Edward out of his stiff jacket and spread a blanket over him to keep him warm. A white handkerchief peeked out of the breast pocket of his vest, and she reached to tuck it back in.

But then her fingers paused their task as she spotted a flicker of brown against the white cloth.

Carefully, she pulled the handkerchief out of the pocket and gasped when she found a lock of hair threatening to fall out. No, not just any lock of hair. *Her* hair. From when she'd gifted it to him on the night of the masquerade.

"You've carried it all this time?" she murmured, unfolding the square cloth to find the lock of hair well-preserved, a faint golden sheen in the small strands of brunette. Perhaps he truly *did* care. Unless he told her differently, she refused to give up hope.

"Stay with me," she whispered one more time as she leaned over him, placing a gentle kiss on his forehead. "We'll get through this. Together."

She swore she felt his hand twitch in hers, and she hoped more than anything he would hold on. If not for himself, then for her and the child she was growing in her womb.

She glanced toward the door just as another nurse shuffled in with more blankets, but no one else lingered outside the door from what she could tell from her vantage point.

If necessary, she would guard Edward from whatever threat wanted him dead. If they dared to try again...

They would have to get through her first.

Chapter Thirteen

QUITE FRANKLY, EDWARD found himself growing tired of waking up in a bed after no recollection of falling asleep in the first place. And in an immense amount of pain at that.

His chest felt heavy, and each breath he took was like the stab of a knife through the ribs.

Slowly, he blinked his eyes open, but his disorientation only grew when he stared up at an unfamiliar ceiling, lying on an unfamiliar cot in an unfamiliar room. Rather than walls of bumpy stone, he faced a flat surface a light green in color.

On the bedside table lay a variety of medical equipment, including an uneaten meal of bread and cheese and a glass of water.

His parched throat begged for the water, and unable to stop himself, he reached for it with a shaky hand, only to find another hand darting out to snatch it first.

He inhaled sharply, only to glance up to find Cedric offering him a sympathetic smile.

"Slowly," his friend cautioned as he helped him drink the lukewarm water. Some of it spilled onto his shirt, but most of it made it down his throat.

"Where am I?" Edward croaked after he finished half the glass and glanced around with bleary, confused eyes.

"The palace infirmary. You collapsed outside. Well, your lung collapsed, too. But the doctor is treating it."

"You've stayed with me this whole time?"

"Of course." He chuckled sheepishly, running a hand over the back of his neck. "I had to be thoroughly inspected before I was allowed to be alone with you, stripped down and changed into new clothes. But I think I've cleared my name. Or at least, I hope."

Confusion swirled in his mind as he tried to make sense of Cedric's words. "I don't understand."

"You were poisoned," the doctor from the palace infirmary—Doctor Clark, if he remembered correctly—said from the doorway. "Actually, it has been an ongoing poisoning for the past year." The man crossed the room and sat in a chair beside his bed. "Do you know anyone who wishes you harm?"

His mouth dropped open as disbelief worked its way into his fatigued body and slow mind. Sleep and disorientation still flitted around his head, his mind finding it difficult to grasp the man's meaning.

"No one would harm me," he insisted in a raspy voice.

But then his lips pressed tightly together as he thought of his sister and how she would sometimes strike him. But poison him? Even she wasn't cruel enough to do something like that. Surely.

The doctor inspected his chest, mouth, eyes, and watched as he took several deep breaths. Next, he set out a variety of ingredients, naming each one out loud as if wanting him to know he wasn't trying to harm him in any way.

"Your fiancée is quite the spirited one, isn't she?" The man glanced at him from the corner of his eye as he began adding ingredients to his mortar. "Wouldn't leave your side until I forced her to step away to get some rest."

"My what?" His confused and troubled mind couldn't catch onto his words, unable to make sense of them.

"Lady Vivienne Winfield." The man continued to watch him as if gauging his reaction while he added several more herbs to a mortar. "She said you proposed. And she accepted."

Did she?

A slow smile crept up on his lips as his thoughts turned to the lovely woman in question. No one made him laugh quite like she did. He could spend hours with her and never tire of her company. And if what the doctor said was true? Then he was the luckiest man in the entire kingdom.

And then his train of thought turned to their fight in the carriage, to her life-altering secret. He wished she would have told him sooner. Then he would have been able to sort out this mess without the uncertainty of his death.

Despite how terrified he felt over the idea of becoming a father, elation also filled him at the new hope of building a life with Vivienne, at building a family. If the doctor was correct, that he'd been poisoned, perhaps he could recover. Maybe he wouldn't die, after all.

"I must see her."

"I'm sure she will show her face soon," the man chuckled, seemingly appeased at his reaction to the unexpected news of their betrothal. "The entire castle is in an uproar. About how you were so excited to propose that you collapsed a lung."

The quick gossip must have been Barnaby's doing. Edward would recognize his friend's meddling handiwork anywhere.

"Ugh," he grunted. "I'm terribly embarrassed."

"Don't be. All the ladies at court are swooning over the romantic notion of it." And then he grimaced as he mashed the ingredients together in a bowl. "Duke Hastings is rather put out. Furious, even. He had planned to propose to the Lady Vivienne, but you beat him to it."

Edward released a long sigh, too exhausted to worry about the aftermath of his actions. "Not a great enemy to have."

"Neither are you, Your Lordship. And he knows it."

Edward found it refreshing that the doctor was rather open with his thoughts and opinions. Especially considering he catered to much of the upper class living within the palace.

Quick footsteps rushed in the direction of the room, and moments later, the door flew open without receiving a knock first. There, on the other side, Vivienne stood panting for air, her brunette hair wild with half of it in an updo and the other half falling out of the pins and around her shoulders.

Doctor Clark chuckled. "Ah, there she is now."

"Edward!" Vivienne gasped, flying to his bedside and grasping his hand. "You're awake. Oh, how worried I've been! I didn't get a wink of sleep when the thought of your suffering plagued me every minute of the night. I was terrified you might never wake. So when one of the nurses sent for me, imagine how fast I ran to see you. Of course, others laughed at me for my haste, but more of a dreamy sigh kind of laugh? Anyway, I am so happy to see you're conscious."

Despite his fatigue, his body reacted to her simple touch by spreading heat through his chest, up his neck, and to his ears.

He didn't get the chance to reply when the doctor instructed him to drink the medicine he'd created. It tasted like something foul, and he grimaced as he coughed and forced it down. But he did so with a flicker of hope. Perhaps he wouldn't die if he wasn't unknowingly consuming poison each day.

"I need to speak with Vivi alone," he said after washing the medicine down with a swig of water.

The other two left, shutting the door closed behind them. He wasted no time before turning to her. "Everyone thinks we're engaged. Did you accept me?"

She sat in the chair the doctor had previously occupied and picked at an errant thread on her dress. "Of course, I did. I would be a hopeless fool not to."

He released a long, relieved sigh, the unease in his heart quieting to a softer joy. "I'm glad."

More distracted fiddling. "To warn you, my mother has become quite involved with the upcoming marriage. She wants to marry us in one week's time," and then she stressed the next part, *"to avoid the heavy snowfalls should we wait longer."*

Or in other words, to marry them quickly to avoid scandal. It seemed her mother knew. Did anyone else?

He decided he didn't care. Whatever happened, he would stay by Vivienne's side. And he hoped rather than succumbing to death after just a few weeks or several months, he might live for much longer once his body recuperated.

He reached for her, needing to touch her, to feel the reassurance of her presence. His fingers grazed her shoulder, and too weak to lift his hand for long, it trailed down her arm and rested over her hand.

"And no one suspects the quick marriage?"

Laughter escaped her, but the worry still lingered in her eyes. She also continued to look anywhere else but at him. "Everyone is too busy thinking our courtship has been overly romantic, the details fed down the gossiping chain by your zealous friends. Well, romanticized details without all the scandal." She laughed and shook her head, staring into her lap.

"How did this become so...widespread?"

She shrugged one shoulder and played with a strand of hair brushing her shoulder. "Barnaby made quite the fuss out of the proposal, spinning a few tales here and there. It's quite the love story in the palace gossiping circle." She bit her lip, her attention fixed on her hair. "Well, I suppose *one-sided* love story. But that doesn't matter to everyone when all they see is what they want to see."

"Vivi," he murmured, reaching to capture her fretting hand and tugging it closer to rest over his heart. "I have loved you since the moment you snapped your heel. There is nothing 'one-sided' about this situation. My only regret is making you feel as if there were."

At last, she lifted her head, tears swimming in her eyes as she bit her quivering lip. "But why the sudden change of heart? Was I not enough? Why did I have to bring this," she nodded to her belly, "into the equation before you finally accepted me?"

The sadness in her eyes drowned him in sorrow. What had he done to her? How could he fix this? "Because it gave me an excuse to be selfish. And for the first time in a while, I have hope."

"You were fully willing to step aside for the duke."

At the mention of the man, Edward's lips thinned and his fist clenched. "Oh, believe me. I have imagined you married to the duke countless times, and each instance makes my blood boil. But I only wanted you to be happy."

"I am happy with you."

His heart caught at the confession, and denying himself no longer, he cupped her around the back of the neck and pulled her into a kiss.

A grunt of surprise escaped her, but then she melted into him, meeting each of his soft kisses with some of her own. His fingers skimmed over the silky tresses of her hair, his unleashed passion giving him the strength he needed to pull her closer until one of her hands braced against the cot beside him.

He deepened the kiss and sighed at the way she dug her fingers into his hair, at the way she whispered words of affection between kisses, at the way her touch set his entire body ablaze.

His childhood best friend was the woman he was going to marry. Never in his life would he have ever seen it coming. But it felt real. It felt right. And most of all, it felt wonderful.

"I love you, Vivienne Winfield," he murmured the moment they broke apart and rested their foreheads together.

A warm tear plopped onto his cheek. He found her hand and pressed it to his chest, trying with all his might to convey his sincerity. He would express his feelings a thousand times if only so she might believe them.

"I love you, Edward Beaumont." She trailed kisses from his temple to his cheek, from his jaw to his neck. "And I'm going to take care of you. Always."

He chuckled but winced when his lungs weren't quite ready for such a thing. "It's never as bad as this. I promise." His thumb caressed the smooth skin on her jaw. "I will have good days and bad. And on the bad days, I simply have to rest more and avoid manual tasks or activities." His gaze fixated on her lips, on the way they curved into a worried frown at his words. "There are more good days than bad."

"And what if you have an episode while I'm away? Who will help you?"

It was endearing the way she worried. But if what the doctor said was true, if they rid his body of the poison and it healed to its former health, then he thought he could manage.

"Cedric is always with me. He's my friend, but he's also paid well to be my shadow."

When the words seemed to appease her, she stroked his hair and kissed his cheek. He'd never thought he'd find himself betrothed, let alone married. He was a lucky man, indeed.

"I told you that you liked my hair," he teased weakly, letting out a long breath and sinking back into his pillows. Fatigue set into his bones once again as the heat from her kiss dissipated from his veins.

"Oh, hush," she laughed, brown eyes sparkling with happiness. And then she said, "Given the nature of our fast-approaching wedding, I have a surprise for you when you gain back your strength. A short little adventure."

"A surprise?" He frowned. "I haven't done anything for you. I don't even have a ring yet." Well, not on him at the moment, at least.

Another laugh, and she lightly shoved his shoulder. "Barnaby spun a tale about how you were too love-struck and frazzled to remember the ring. Prepare yourself for unholy amounts of ribbing."

"I'm certain there will be plenty of that from what I've been told."

She kissed him lightly on the lips one last time. "Get some rest. I have to oversee wedding preparations, but there is a guard stationed outside the infirmary door just in case."

"You are a dream, Vivi."

"Oh…" She waved away his comment with a flip of her hand. "If you are trying to get me to stay, it's working. So stop it."

A grin spread across his face as she blew him one last kiss before disappearing from the room.

"Cedric," he called, and moments later, his servant entered and dipped at the waist in a slight bow.

"Yes, Your Lordship?"

"I need a ring."

Chapter Fourteen

"IS THIS ABSOLUTELY NECESSARY?"

Edward held a wooden cane in his hands, staring down at the thing with a disgruntled frown.

Vivienne smoothed her hands over her fiancé's chest to remove a couple wrinkles from his vest that had managed to sneak past her careful screening. She wanted the surprise to go perfectly. Mostly because she wanted to give Edward every happiness possible. But also because it was an important day.

"The Mother Goddess knows I can try to catch you if you fall, but I'm quite certain we'll *both* end up sprawled on the floor." She patted his hand resetting atop the cane and smiled. "Besides, your body is still healing." Once again, she nodded her head toward the wooden wheelchair resting against the wall. "Of course, I'd prefer you in the chair—"

"I will not lower myself to wheeling about like a cripple. I can walk just fine."

She tsked, shaking her head. "A bit testy today, aren't we?"

"I'm nervous."

"For what?" She laughed as they walked side by side out of the infirmary and into the quiet hallway, Cedric trailing several paces behind. "You don't know what we're doing yet."

His frown remained as he hobbled at her side, clearly needing the cane more than he cared to admit. She wanted to kiss the frown away, as adorable as she found it. "I assume we're on a jaunt to *meet with the parents*. I'm still waiting for your father to impale me."

"At this point, you are a beloved member of court," she teased, gently elbowing him in the ribs. "He wouldn't dare."

He glanced at her, his gaze trailing over the beaded and embroidered scarf she wore.

"Is that the one?" he asked, his worries momentarily distracted by her clothing ensemble. "The scarf you said you never wore because you didn't want to ruin it."

She smiled as she lifted both ends of the beautiful item to admire the careful stitches and the skillful craftsmanship. "How can I say it's well-loved if I hide it away? You inspired me, Edward. After seeing how much you loved your book…"

His mouth turned up at the corners as he trailed the scarf between his fingers. "I can see why you love it so much. It's unique. Just like the woman who wears it."

"Oh," she gently swatted his arm, a bashful smile on her face, "you certainly know how to make a grown woman feel special."

But then she stopped short in the hallway, her eyes flashing open with fear as she realized something she hadn't considered before. "How will your heart react to a surprise?"

"I'll be fine, Vivi." This time, he turned his head and smiled. The sight of it weakened her knees and nearly made *her* feel like the one who might collapse. "I'm not quite as fragile as you are led to believe."

"I love you," she breathed. But then her hand flew to her heated cheek as his grin widened, and the smug look that simultaneously challenged her and brought out her playful side emerged.

"My, my, Vivienne Winfield. You sure do know how to make a grown man feel rather special."

She chuckled nervously, the heat in her face refusing to abate. "This feels surreal. Everything about this is surreal. It's almost like if I close my eyes, I'll wake up and nothing will be the same."

"I believe you are thinking of tomorrow." He teasingly pinched her side. "When you will wake up, and it will be our wedding day."

They stopped in front of a set of large double doors with a servant standing on each side. Although she was usually a confident person, she needed the reassurance of his contentedness with his lot, especially when she'd so forcefully shoved it onto his shoulders.

"Are you happy?" she whispered to prevent the servants from overhearing.

He reached out to her but seemed to think better of it when the movement caused him to wobble on his legs. In an equal whisper, he said, "Remember in my letter when I said these past few months have been the best of my life?" She nodded, and he continued. "I think the past few days, even being bedridden, has topped it all. I am very happy."

A relieved breath escaped on her exhale. "I'm so glad." And then she laughed, saying in a louder voice, "Now, I hope that doesn't change in ten seconds from now."

With a gesture of her hand, she motioned for the guards to open the doors leading into the smaller ballroom within the palace. And then a chorus of clapping and congratulations slammed into them, effectively taking Edward off guard enough to stun him with silence.

When his feet froze to the floor, she slipped her arm into his and guided him into the room where nearly every member of court had shown up to congratulate them on their engagement, including the king and queen of Edilann.

A sea of colorful skirts surrounded them. Ladies with fans. Gentleman with cravats to match. And at the front of the ensemble stood her mother and father, each of them beaming with smiles to reflect her own.

"What is this?" Edward finally stammered beside her.

She squeezed his bicep. "It's our engagement party."

One by one, guests approached to offer their congratulations, and when Edward finally recovered from the shock, he conversed with them excitedly as if he'd been locked in a tower for most of his life, and he'd only recently escaped for a breath of fresh air.

Oh wait…

Vivienne remained close, often touching his arm or hand, shoulder or waist, reflecting the truthful appearance of how happy she was. Nothing could take away her joy of the moment. Absolutely nothing.

At least until Duke Hastings approached. No mask or polite decorum could hide the fiery glint of anger in the man's eyes. His fists clenched. His nostrils flared.

"This was supposed to be *my* engagement party," the man hissed, pointing a menacing finger in Edward's face.

The entire room quieted. Tension thickened in the air until it became difficult to breathe.

She caught onto Edward's hand and gripped his fingers when she feared a fight breaking out in the middle of the ballroom. He couldn't possibly win a brawl. Especially not in his condition.

But to his credit, he remained calm as he gave her fingers a reassuring squeeze. "Duke Hastings, leave some engagement parties for the rest of us." He then dipped his head. "Your Grace."

The entire room burst into nervous laughter as if unable to hold back their amusement at Edward's ribbing jest. The duke had been married two other times, and relief washed over her at the thought of narrowly avoiding being his third.

"I will never forget this, Beaumont," he seethed. And just when Vivienne feared he might strike Edward, he turned abruptly on his heel and strode out of the room.

Silence ensued the moment the doors slammed closed.

"Well," Mother cut in with a bright smile, effectively slicing through the thick tension in the room. "Let's enjoy the music and refreshments, shall we?"

As the quartet struck up soft background music from the corner, everyone crowded closer around the two of them, gossipping whispers already circling through the crowd.

"Lord Beaumont!" Lady Whitaker called. "Why would you race the duke to propose first?"

Everyone within the immediate vicinity leaned closer as if to hear his response.

"I had no idea he was going to propose," he likely answered honestly. "I've been planning to propose to Vivienne for weeks."

"Then why have you waited until now?"

"Because I was waiting for the right moment." He smiled in a self-deprecating manner as he glanced down at her. "I don't think I quite pulled off the execution."

Another rumble of laughter flitted through the crowd. And oh, how she wanted to steal him away to the balcony and kiss him tenderly, away from watching eyes.

One of the next people to approach was Edward's uncle Maxwell. The man smiled and heartily shook Edward's hand and gently cupped hers. "V.W.," he said, chuckling as he shook his head. "Vivienne Winfield. I should have known."

She glanced at Edward from the corner of his eye but he only shrugged sheepishly.

The man continued, "I am so happy my nephew has found someone. You make him happy. So very happy."

Her father approached next and handed Edward a red and blue jewel-encrusted dagger within a golden sheath. Her eyes smarted at the meaning behind the gift. It was an heirloom, staying within the family for many generations.

"Your parents were good friends of ours," her father said with a suspicious croak to his words. "There is no one I would rather give her to than you."

Edward's tense shoulders visibly relaxed, though his hand shook as if he found the task of holding onto his cane difficult. "I will take care of her. I promise you." And then his eyebrows shot up as he patted his breast pockets, until finally, a glint of something small caught onto the candlelight in the room.

"I remembered the ring," he called out as he held up a small black ring with red rubies that looked like roses surrounded by black, metal leaves. A chorus of laughter echoed through the audience while her hand flew to her heart. It looked just like...

Her wonderful fiancé slipped it onto her finger, and she could have wept at how perfectly it fit, as if it were made just for her.

"Oh, Edward, it's lovely," she said as she held out her hand to admire the ring. And then more quietly, she said, "It greatly resembles the dress I wore to the masquerade..."

"How could I forget?"

She lifted her gaze, the audience chattering excitedly to lend them a small measure of privacy in their conversation. "You couldn't possibly have acquired this within the space of a few days."

He leaned more heavily on his cane as if he struggled to stand, speaking close to her ear. "The night of the masquerade, you were everything I never knew I wanted. I had the ring commissioned long before today." He chuckled before adding, "Even if I wasn't sure I would ever marry with my condition."

Her eyes smarted. "I could kiss you right now."

"Don't do it," he warned playfully. "You'll cause a scandal." But then he shrugged. "Or do it. What's one more?"

Temptation burned with the passion staring back at her through his eyes. She might have kissed him if Cedric hadn't approached with a soft armchair the moment Edward's legs collapsed on him.

The servant made the collapse look natural, as if Edward had planned to sit right then. No one seemed to notice, and she tried not to make a big deal of it as she also took the chair another servant offered to remain by Edward's side.

She glanced at him from the corner of her eye as he continued to converse with members of court, worry knotting her stomach. Fatigue rested heavy beneath his eyes. But the beaming smile on his face spoke volumes at how much he enjoyed being out and about in society.

When they married, she would make sure he had plenty of opportunities to leave the house and attend social functions. Clara would no longer rule him with an iron fist.

She inhaled sharply, her eyes snapping wide open when she realized Clara was not in attendance, even though Edward's uncle had shown his face, giving them gifts and one of the heartiest congratulations of them all.

Could Clara…

No, it couldn't possibly be true. She would never have harmed her own brother, right?

But then she realized just how much she could gain by Edward's death. She would be the lady of the house, and her son would become the new viscount.

"Edward," she murmured, but her voice was quickly drowned out by the festivities. She tapped on his arm, drawing his attention for mere moments before someone swooped in and commandeered her attention instead. Therefore, she pasted a smile on her face and decided to wait until after the party to bring up the worries churning through her stomach.

As long as Edward's attempted murderer was out there, he wasn't safe. And she didn't think she could close her eyes at night knowing he could still be a target at any moment.

However, after the party ended, her friends and sisters whisked her away for a small get-together of their own in their family suite, not giving her the chance to speak to Edward privately like she wished. His friends also stole him away, effectively separating them for the remainder of the night.

Instead of expressing her frustration at the setback, she snatched a piece of parchment and a quill from the table to write him a letter.

My Sweet Edward,

Time has passed quickly, but not quickly enough. Our wedding is only one more day away, but it also seems like ages. I believe fate has brought us together, and I know with a certainty it can never tear us apart.

You gifted me your most prized possession, and I have been reading it every night before bed. I read it to you in the infirmary for hours each day, hoping that the sound of my voice could help you heal.

One of my favorite stories is The Singing Bone. I ask that you read it to remember me in our short time apart.

I'm looking forward to standing beside you at the altar.

Truly Yours,
Vivi

And then she tucked the letter inside the tale of *The Singing Bone* and gave it to a servant to deliver to Edward. The tale was about a jealous brother who killed his younger brother to take credit for the boor the younger one had killed. By doing so, he was given the princess's hand in marriage, receiving recognition and renown. At least until the horn made of the dead boor's bones sang the truth of what happened to the boy.

If Edward heeded her warning about her suspicions, then he would be on his guard.

Yet, she couldn't help but pace about the room and wring her hands, even as her sisters fussed over the planning for her hair and wardrobe for the upcoming wedding.

Tomorrow. They would be married tomorrow.

It was only one more night apart. Edward was safe. She needn't worry.

Surely.

But as she pulled back the drapes to gaze at the darkened world outside, the half moon glittering in the night sky, her heart steadily sank to her toes.

If Clara didn't want this wedding to happen…

She'd find a way to stop it.

Chapter Fifteen

"STOP IT!" EDWARD LAUGHED as he shoved his friend, Charles, in the shoulder but nearly missed, narrowingly avoiding falling flat on his face. "I've had enough of all your teasing for one night."

He hobbled through the hallways of the palace with the remaining strength in his body. True, he should have rested more considering it was the night before the wedding, but at least his friends had allowed him to sit as they'd played cards and games and regaled each other with memories of the past.

Two of his friends, Charles and Barnaby, were already married, and now Edward would be the third. But their friendship hadn't missed a single step because of it.

"Someone has to do it," Tobie said as he roughed up his hair. "After tomorrow, you'll be a married man."

Flickering torchlight lining each side of the hallway cast shadows across the walls, creating a sudden sense of uneasiness as his new, temporary room came into sight. Two guards stood on either side of the door, staring forward, each wearing leather armor. Their leather helmets hid most of their faces, which only amplified his anxiety.

But as Barnaby squeezed his shoulder and ribbed him again about this being his last night alone, he forced a tight smile, reminding himself he was safe here. No harm would come to him.

His friends bid him farewell, and he sent Cedric away to get sleep, promising he would send for him if absolutely necessary.

Heart pounding with discomfort, he approached the two guards with his room key in hand. Neither glanced his way, but one of them held out a familiar book with an envelope tucked inside the pages.

"For Your Lordship," the man said with a brief nod. "From the Lady Vivienne."

Edward eagerly took the book from him, thanked him, and disappeared inside his room. His fingers trembled with excitement as he lit his lantern, bathing the room in a soft orange glow.

When his legs refused to hold his weight any longer, he sank onto the soft mattress of his bed and didn't hesitate a moment longer as he slipped the envelope out of the book, broke the seal, and read the letter within.

At first, he smiled at her sweet words. But slowly, his smile melted into a confused frown when she mentioned a rather dreary fairy tale. Her favorite? He knew without a doubt it was one of her *least* favorites.

I ask that you read it to remember me in our short time apart.

"Can I not read it tomorrow?" he chuckled to himself. "I'm bone tired."

But as he loosened his cravat with the intention of sleeping fully clothed when he was too exhausted to dress himself down, he glanced again at the book and the letter keeping the page bookmarked.

With a sigh, he carefully opened the worn-out pages of the tome, his eyes traveling over the words but his mind not making sense of them in its weary state. Surely, this could wait a day or two, even if he wanted to give Vivienne the world. Including this very simple request.

He started to close the book when he noticed one of the letters was darker than the rest, as if someone had intentionally traced over it with ink.

C.

His eyebrows drew together when another letter on the next page looked similar. *L.* He knew for a fact that he hadn't drawn over it himself. Had Vivienne? Or perhaps he hadn't read this story enough to realize it had always looked this way.

Sure enough, several more letters throughout the story were colored the same. Sporadic. Without a pattern. Almost like a game. Like a...

Hidden message.

Quickly, he turned back to the beginning and began stringing the letters together in his mind. C. L. A. R. A.

What did that spell? Was he missing a letter? Were there any other letters hidden throughout the pages of the other stories?

But as he searched for similar letters, he found none, which brought him back to the ones he'd discovered. It wasn't like any word he knew. It was closer to nonsense than an actual word or phrase. Kind of like...

A name.

His blood ran cold as he finally pieced together what the message said. Clara. His sister. And considering the story he'd found her name in…

Vivienne thought Clara was his would-be killer.

"No, no stop!" someone shouted from the corridor.

A gurgled grunt, followed by a thump in the hallway, snapped his attention toward his closed door. His heart shot to his throat. He stumbled to his feet, blindly grasping for anything to use as a weapon on the nearby table until his fingers clasped around the hilt of the jeweled dagger given to him by Vivienne's father.

He wasn't a weapons enthusiast like his friend, Charles. He didn't even keep knives on his person like Barnaby. He had books and stars, neither of which would help him right now.

His pulse pounded through his veins as his grip tightened on his dagger, not knowing if the blade within the sheath was sharp or dull.

With his other hand, he patted his pockets for his key and finally found it in his trousers. Had he locked the door? He couldn't recall if he'd had the chance in his excitement to read Vivienne's letter.

Clara? the voice inside his head trembled to ask.

He was bigger than her. Stronger, too. She would never be able to get close enough to injure him if he fought back. But…that was on a good day. His body was still healing.

The door rattled. Locked.

Panic consumed him as he tucked his dagger into his waistband and tugged the sheets off his bed. His hands shook as he worked to tie them together and then next around the leg of his bed.

The door handle rattled again, this time sounding as if something metal scraped against it.

Rather than staying to find out who the person was on the opposite end of the door, Edward threw open the window, inhaling sharply as cold air smashed into his face. He grabbed onto the bed sheets and tossed one leg over the side of the sill, followed by the other, until he scaled down the palace wall with shaky, unstable limbs.

Riiiip!

Edward cried out as he found himself suspended in the air for mere moments until the fabric caught again. His body smashed against the side of the stone wall, violently jarring him enough for his grip to fail him, and he plummeted the rest of the way to the ground.

He groaned as he pushed himself to his hands and knees onto half-frozen mud. His entire body ached from the impact, and a shivering chill set into his bones.

But somehow, he managed to climb to his feet and glance up at the open window far above him. The blood drained from his face as a head peeked out, their attention quickly honing on him. They wore a leather guardsman helmet that shrouded their features, but the person's shoulders were distinctly masculine.

If it wasn't Clara, then who was after him? An assassin?

The man threw a rope over the side of the window. Edward gasped as he turned and sprinted in the opposite direction, not entirely knowing where he was going when he wasn't familiar with the palace grounds. In the extreme darkness of midnight, he quickly lost the path. His clothing caught on brambles like teeth trying to snap him up in its maw.

The first thing he should have done was find a palace guard. But considering one now chased him through tall trees and unforgiving branches, he didn't dare turn back toward the castle, not knowing who was a friend and who was an enemy.

Feet crashed through the underbrush behind him, gaining on him by the second. Breaths wheezed in and out of his weak lungs. His heart beat far too quickly, threatening to collapse on him and spill him onto the forest floor. Weakness plagued his body. But somehow, he kept running as fast as his ailing body would carry him.

Something slammed into him from behind, hardly giving him any warning before he crashed to the ground, skidding over mud and roots and hidden cobblestone.

He rolled over onto his back, only to halt when something cold pressed against his neck.

"You were always slower than the other children," a voice snarled above him. "It seems as if nothing has changed."

Edward wheezed, his fingers desperately clawing for escape. But the blade against his throat pressed hard enough for him to cease his efforts. Quick, frosty breaths escaped his mouth, clouding his view of the man pinning him down, threatening him with a sharp dagger.

"It never had to end this messily," his attacker growled. "But now you give me no choice."

The man shifted as if he were about to drag the weapon across his throat, but then something else tackled him to the ground.

Edward gasped in air the moment the blade left his neck. He rolled onto his feet and struggled to stand. For a moment, his heart stopped as he found Vivienne standing several paces away in her nightgown and bare feet, a bloody knife in her hand. His attacker was doubled over, the back of his shoulder covered in blood.

"Vivi!" He scrambled toward her and reached out a hand, but before he touched her, the attacker launched to his feet, grabbed Vivienne around the neck, and pressed the knife against her throat.

No! he screamed in his mind. *Not her. Not her!*

"Stop!" he cried, lifting a cautioning hand. "Release her. You can have me. Please. *Please.*"

Edward's fingers brushed against the dagger he wore tucked in his waistband, but he didn't draw it. Not yet. Not while Vivienne's life was in danger.

"But now there's a witness, isn't there?" The man squeezed her tighter around the shoulders until she grunted in pain.

Suddenly, Edward's blood ran cold, his jaw hanging agape as he finally recognized the man's face, the man's voice. "Uncle Maxwell?" he gasped.

His uncle reached for his helmet, tugged it off his head, and threw it to the ground, revealing wild, murderous eyes and a nest of black hair. He no longer resembled the kind and patient uncle he'd known his entire life.

"Why…why…?" Edward shook his head, glancing between his uncle and the dagger he pressed to Vivienne's throat. "What vexes you to do such a thing?"

"Have you not pieced it together, nephew?" The man released a deranged laugh, his wild eyes catching a glint of the moonlight overhead. "I have slowly been poisoning you for a year now. For as many books as you read, you are not very bright."

"Run, Edward," Vivienne said in a strangled voice, her gaze flicking from his face to the path to the left of him. "Do not give this sick bastard the satisfaction of listening to another word he says!" And then she screamed as Maxwell pulled back on her hair and angled the blade so dangerously that even the smallest movement might spell her death.

Panic consumed him, dread piling like dead bodies in its wake. He took a single step forward but stopped when Maxwell shook his head ever so slightly.

"I want your title," his uncle growled. "It's mine. It should have always been mine. Your father was sick, just like you. He should have died. But he didn't. At least not before his wife birthed a son."

"But you wouldn't be the heir. James would."

Maxwell tugged harder on Vivienne's hair until tears of pain leaked out of her eyes. "Little children come by accidents all the time. It wouldn't have been difficult to dispose of James next. But oh, how I would *grieve.*" The man's unhinged laughter sent a chill up Edward's spine.

"Why?" he rasped, fearful of advancing any farther and risking Vivienne getting nicked by the blade. "You lead a good life. Why do you need mine?"

"I have nothing," his uncle hissed. "Your vile father took half my trading ships when they went to find a cure for your so-called ailment. And you know what? They never returned. And neither did my ships."

Grief and guilt cut him deeper than any knife could. "I was a boy then. What could I have done to sway them against their decision to leave? They were trying to preserve their line."

Yet, the guilt had eaten him alive for many years until he'd finally forgiven himself for what he couldn't control.

"And what of your other trading ships?" Edward asked, desperately glancing from the terror in Vivienne's eyes to the knife at her throat. A chill rapidly climbed up his arms, soaking him to the bone. "You are still a wealthy man."

"Not anymore. The money has dried up in failed investments. I can't start over. I need your title and your wealth."

"By killing me?" His weak body lost its footing, and he shifted just enough to catch himself on the nearby trunk of a tree. "What have you done to Clara?"

"Nothing yet. I might take pity on her poor soul and marry her off to someone who will take her off my hands. Or I might not. I haven't quite decided."

Edward's gaze darted toward Vivienne once more. His uncle hadn't killed her yet like he'd tried to do to him. There must be a reason. "I'm sick. I'll exaggerate just how much to the king and forsake my title. I'll move several leagues away if it appeases you. Just let her go. I beg you."

Maxwell's features relaxed, although he didn't loosen his grip on Vivienne. He smiled, but it held more menace than amiability. "I will be sure to mourn the hardest at your closed-casket funeral. My poor nephew and his fiancée assassinated by Armandy soldiers on a midnight tryst." He reached into his pocket and threw several golden medallions with the Armandy crest to the ground. "What a tragic love story."

His uncle flexed his arm as if prepping for the kill.

Edward had never moved so quickly in his life as he launched himself forward.

The quick action seemed to take Maxwell off guard. The faint hesitation lent him mere moments to do what must be done.

One moment he stood by the tree, and the next, he unsheathed his knife and thrust it into his uncle's stomach.

The other man grunted. Blood spilled out of the wound. His grip loosened on Vivienne, giving her the chance to slip out of the confinement of his blade.

But then the remaining strength in Edward's body failed him as he collapsed to his knees. Maxwell's expression contorted with rage. He swung his dagger at Edward's head. Vivienne screamed.

Rather than experiencing blinding pain before the darkness of death, Maxwell's blade caught on another in a screech of metal. Blindingly fast, the newcomer disarmed his uncle, and when Maxwell unsheathed a second dagger from his belt and attempted a second stab, the other man impaled him through the chest with his sword.

A grunt escaped his uncle's lips moments before he crashed onto his side and lay unmoving on the cold, hard ground.

Edward stared in disbelief at the uncle he had looked up to his entire life, at the man who had played with him and laughed with him and made him feel as if he weren't quite so alone. How could his heart ache so fiercely for a man who had tried to kill him several times and attempted to murder the woman he loved?

"Edward!" Vivienne gasped, pulling him out of his shocked daze as she threw her arms around his neck. "Are you injured? Let me see you." She pulled back just enough to inspect his face, his chest, his arms. And when she seemed satisfied that no blade had touched him, she embraced him yet again.

He blinked dazedly as his gaze found the man who had ended his uncle's life. He wore an Edilann guardsman uniform, the blue of his cloak standing out against the pale moonlight as he cleaned his weapon on dead grass.

Only twice before had Edward seen the burly man with brown hair and wide-set shoulders. Gilberd Keats had saved young Prince Sterling's life years ago and had been offered the position as the personal bodyguard to the prince himself. What was he doing outside at midnight in his uniform?

As if hearing his unspoken thoughts, the man nodded his head toward a young boy with wide eyes peeking his head out from behind a tree. "He decided to sneak out. Again. He might have just saved both of your sorry arses by doing so."

Vivienne gasped and quickly bowed to Prince Sterling. Edward couldn't find the energy to do so as well, especially as Gilberd grabbed onto his arm and hoisted him to his feet. He barely remained standing when the shock of his uncle's death and the weakness in his body threatened to collapse him.

Gilberd didn't stay by his side but rather approached his uncle's body, crouching down to examine him. Edward had to look away. It didn't seem real. All this time, Maxwell had been the one to poison him? He suspected his original doctor was somehow involved, too. His uncle had confirmed Clara's innocence, and he felt immensely relieved that he at least had one family member he could trust.

"Forgive me," Vivienne said, blinking rapidly. "I thought it was Clara. I was close. But not correct."

He reached for her hand and squeezed her fingers. "Your warning gave me enough time to be on my guard." His thumb caressed the back of her hand when she began shivering as if the chill only recently set in after the shock. "How did you find me?"

"I saw you from my window. I couldn't sleep. I've been so worried about you." She covered her face with her free hand. "You put me in a panic when I saw you fall. And again when you started running. I should have brought guards. But there was no time."

"You saved my life, Vivi. Had you come even a second later…"

But then he inhaled sharply as he remembered her bare feet. He stooped to pick her up and relieve her feet from the frigid ground. But when he nearly collapsed the both of them, he grunted and shook his head, setting her back down.

"Nuh uh, this is not happening. My body is too exhausted." Rather, he slipped his shoes off and helped her into them. They adorably dwarfed her feet.

Next, he took his dress coat off and draped it over her shoulders.

"You'll catch a cold," Vivienne protested.

"A cold is the least of my concerns right now." And then he pulled her closer until she fit securely in his arms, his chin resting on the top of her head. "You are the bravest woman I know."

She tipped her head up to look at him and bit her lip, her immense worry still staring back at him. "Should we postpone the wedding?"

After her desperation to wed before she started showing, she sure didn't seem to care now. Not after what had happened. But keeping her safe was of the utmost importance to him, which included the sphere of her reputation and happiness. "No. We won't let this ruin our day."

Gilberd interrupted them as he gestured with his arm for them to follow the path back to the palace. "I'll have other guards take care of this. I saw the entirety of what happened, so I can add an honest and detailed testimony. We'll inspect your room, Lord Beaumont, and find evidence against Sir Maxwell." And as they walked with the young prince trailing beside them, the guard turned to Vivienne. "Did I see you tonight? Or are you safely tucked in bed?"

Edward glanced at Prince Sterling as Gilberd said this. Hiding information from the monarchy was one thing. But what made Sterling an exception? The two almost seemed like friends with a fifteen-year or so age gap.

"Tell it how it happened," she finally answered. "I likely was not the only witness."

Another worry crept up for the young boy, almost an adolescent now. He was likely still innocent of this world. "He should not have seen that," Edward murmured, watching as Prince Sterling kicked a rock across the path and lifted his head to gaze at the stars with a contemplative expression.

The guard released a long breath and glanced at the prince. "It's not the first time the prince has witnessed death. He'll be all right."

They reached the palace, and Edward gave Vivienne one last embrace as Gilberd sent Sterling back to sleep and alerted guards about what had happened. Edward was bone weary, but he could not sleep when his family member was dead. All because he'd wanted his title.

He'd offered everything. Maxwell could have had his title and his money. But he'd brought this on himself. He'd chosen death over mercy.

Only minutes later, Gilberd returned with a grave look on his face. "One of the men guarding your room is injured, stabbed with the same weapon Maxwell had tried to use on you."

Vivienne's hand flew to her mouth. "Will he live?"

"He might. He's recovering in the infirmary as we speak." Then the man turned to speak to several other guards.

How could his uncle do this? Of course, money and fame made some men delirious with desire, enough to steal and murder. But he could hardly connect the man tonight with the man of his past.

"I need to return home," he murmured in Vivienne's ear as guards flitted around them, their activity drawing the attention from other nobles as well who wandered into the corridors with confused, sleepy expressions while wearing their night clothes. "Clara needs to know what happened."

"What if someone else tries to kill you?" she asked through chattering teeth.

"The person who wanted me dead is gone. I'll take guards with me, too." He kissed her on the forehead and lowered his voice. "Wait for me at the altar. I promise I will be there."

She nodded mutely as she handed him back his shoes and coat, replacing them with a thick, wool blanket instead. "Be safe, Edward."

He lifted her hand and kissed the finger with his ring hugging it, conveying all the sincerity of the love in his soul with the single action.

And then he tried not to glance back at her over his shoulder as Cedric helped him to a waiting carriage to take him back home in the darkness. He wasn't sure he could leave the palace if he did.

Chapter Sixteen

THE CONVERSATION WITH Clara had been filled with tears, honesty, and brutal heartache as they conversed in the late hours of the night in the drawing room round a lantern and late-night refreshments neither of them touched.

"I had no idea, Edward," she sniffed, wiping another tear with a wet handkerchief. "I never would have given you those elixirs if..."

"You didn't know the doctor was hired by Maxwell. How could you have?"

"But I feel responsible." Her shoulders slumped. Shadows jumped across her face in time with the flickering flames from the lantern. "I've been a mess since Emerson left me and James. I was scared. Our parents were gone. You were still young. You were sick, and there was a household to run. I was terrified and overwhelmed. I did what I thought was best for you under the circumstances. But..." Another sniff. "I feel awful for the times I have yelled at you, the times I have struck you. I'm sure I could have found a better way to handle things, to trust you more, rather than locking you in your room each night. Please forgive me."

Never in his life had he seen Clara in this light. So vulnerable. So heartbroken. So defeated.

"I do forgive you."

She continued speaking, her hand covering her face when she seemed to give up on the amount of tears flowing from her eyes. "It was difficult to watch you with Vivienne. I could immediately see the strong connection you shared. But it wasn't fair. I'm the one who has been working so hard, so tirelessly, and you get rewarded." She released a shuddering sigh. "I know my jealousy was wrong, and I feel awful about it. Please forgive me."

"You already asked for forgiveness, and I have already given it." He slowly reached across the space between them and hesitantly touched her shoulder. She stiffened when he gave it a brief squeeze. "Do you not like Vivi?"

"Oh, I do like her." She laughed miserably. "I am so envious of her, too. I have been trying to catch the duke's eye for years, to hopefully give myself a new beginning. And she swoops in and grabs his attention effortlessly." She dabbed at her eyes again. "I know I am not as beautiful as her, not as striking."

"But you *are*," he insisted. "You just aren't bold enough."

"I am undeserving of such happiness. I have treated you so poorly. How can I ever make things up to you?"

Edward had never been one to hold a grudge, and forgiveness came all too easily, even for people who probably didn't deserve it. But Clara was his sister. He wanted to see her happy. "If we can maintain a better relationship with one another, perhaps that's all the redemption you need."

Tears clung to his sister's eyelashes, and it was as if his words flew right over her head. "Please don't abandon me. Please don't throw me out after you marry."

He had never planned on taking away her home. But now that she planted the idea in his head... "You have been so sad since your husband left you."

"What does that have to do with—"

"Do you want to marry again?"

"Well...I..." The rosy blush on her cheeks became visible in the dim light. "I am not what the duke prefers."

Edward shook his head, grunting as he struggled to stand with his cane helping to support his weight. He dug through drawers on the opposite side of the room until he found the box Vivienne had left behind—likely on purpose, too—the one containing the ruby necklace gifted from Duke Hastings.

"It's time for you to be bold, Clara." He grinned from ear to ear as he held the strand of red gems out to her. He'd found a way to make his sister happy while removing her from the premises entirely. "We are going to return the duke's necklace. Just follow my lead."

Vivienne paced back and forth, back and forth in her stunning green and cream wedding gown with a fitted bodice, long, lacy sleeves, and skirts that glimmered when they caught the light just right. It reminded her of the spring thaw after a relentless winter. Coupled with a crown of pine needles and winter florals, she felt beautiful in this dress.

But only one thing was missing—the groom.

"Are you sure he's not dead?" Vivienne choked, shaking out her hands to relieve some of the tension from her fingers. "An assassin hasn't finished him off on his way over? He's thirty minutes late."

"He's coming," her father reassured from where he casually lounged on a chair outside the chapel, his sword resting on his lap. "A servant sent word he was on his way. Besides…" He patted the weapon, the dangerous glint of a war captain in his eye. "I don't think he would dare jilt my darling little girl on her wedding day."

"Jilting is one thing. Dying is another."

Earlier that morning, her father had personally led the search for Edward's previous doctor. It had taken a couple hours to track him down, but finally they'd found him trying to flee the kingdom, the ship about to set sail. He would be tried for his crimes against Edward and his other patients. But her father reassured the man would be locked away for a very long time.

"Give him ten more minutes," her father said, his foot bouncing against his knee. "He probably needs them to climb the stairs alone."

"This isn't funny, Papa!" She swatted his shoulder, but he only laughed. "Collapsed lungs are a very serious thing."

His smile disappeared, but she still spotted the corner of his mouth twitching as if he tried to hold it back. "He'll come."

Vivienne turned to the window and gazed out toward the road, searching for any signs of his carriage rolling toward the palace. She forced herself not to touch her belly when she held in the bile wanting to escape. It was not easy to hide the pregnancy. But they were almost there. Almost to the altar. Where they should have been from the beginning.

Please hurry, she begged. *I can hardly stand to wait any longer.*

―❦―

"So close now, Eddie," Clara reassured. "You're almost there."

But unable to hold himself up any longer, Edward slumped down on the stone staircase leading into the castle, the remaining stairs taunting him with jeers and laughter. There were too many. He couldn't do it.

"I need to rest for a moment."

Over the last several days, he'd noticed his energy returning. His heart episodes became less frequent. His body and mind didn't feel quite so fatigued. The palace doctor said it was a good sign, and that he would likely recover all the way from his poisoning. But it would still take some time to heal, especially for his lung.

Before he could gasp for another breath, two people grabbed him beneath the arms and hoisted him up the rest of the staircase, only for him to discover it was Barnaby and Charles with Tobie trailing behind. He couldn't help but laugh at his weakness, even as his heart warmed with gratitude.

At the top of the stairs, they placed him back on his feet but heavily supported his weight.

"You were taking ages!" Barnaby cried. "We were on our way to hand deliver you to the altar ourselves. We never thought your delay was because you couldn't make it up the stairs."

"I was doing just fine," Edward jested, brushing a piece of lint off his dress jacket. But as a servant rushed forward with a glass of water, he downed the entire thing in a few gulps and handed back the glass. "I'll be there. I need to quickly take care of one more item of business."

"All right," Tobie tsked, wagging a finger at him. "But if you're even five more minutes, we'll drag you by the scruff."

His friends disappeared down the hallway, and Edward took a moment to straighten his clothing before rounding another corner with his sister in tow. Duke Hastings sat in a chair, a disgruntled expression on his face.

"Don't miss the wedding," Edward murmured quietly to Clara.

"I won't," she promised, out of breath and clearly nervous when her hands kept wringing over gloved fingers.

"What is this about, Beaumont?" the duke growled as he stood. "Why did you want to meet?"

"Just a simple social visit. You remember my sister, Clara."

Unbothered by the man's attitude, Edward guided Clara forward, and she hastily dipped into a curtsy. She touched the Duke's ruby necklace clasped around her neck and glanced shyly at the man. "I am flattered over the gift you sent me, Duke Hastings. You have such fine taste in jewelry."

"I did what? No, they weren't for you. They were for..." But then he trailed off, blinking slowly as his gaze took in his sister as if looking at her in a new light. She looked beautiful today, wearing a daring red dress and a hairdo that had taken a servant two hours to complete. Red was a striking color against her black hair. Striking and bold. Which was exactly what she needed to be today.

And then Hastings' expression softened, and Edward didn't miss the hint of hope in his eyes. "Ah, yes. The gift for Lady Clara." He cleared his throat. "I am so glad you like them.

ADORINGLY, EDWARD

You know, they were imported from across the seas from this beautiful city called Valhedra." The man offered Clara his arm, and his voice moved farther out of reach as they ventured down the hallway together. Over her shoulder, his sister mouthed *thank you*.

He simply smiled, wanting to see her happy. Perhaps their sibling relationship could still be mended. It would likely take time, but he finally had hope.

But then his eyes widened as he spun around and quickened his pace down the hallway until he turned the corner and entered the corridor leading toward the back entrance of the palace chapel.

His heart jumped to his throat when he spotted his beautiful bride pacing back and forth before the window, dressed in a stunning green and cream gown with golden accents in the embroidery.

His mouth dried. His skin flushed. Her dress was beautiful. But the woman wearing it managed to outshine it.

His gaze traveled down her curled hair flowing over her shoulders and to the foresty crown lying on top of her head. Emotion caught in his throat when he spotted the necklace of pine cones he'd made for her weaved into the crown as if she were a forest nymph, her beauty next to none.

Behind her, the warlord nodded in Edward's direction, and a moment later, Vivienne spun around to face him. Relief spilled over her features as he approached and kissed her cheek.

"You look absolutely ravishing." He took her hand and spun her in a slow circle, admiring the way the dress flowed around her with the movement.

"Edward!" she giggled, playfully swatting his shoulder. "You ought not to see the bride before the wedding. Where have you been?"

"I was occupied."

She placed her hands on her hips, bringing his attention to the short, lacy gloves covering each delicate finger. "Too occupied to attend your own wedding? My mind worked through every possible terrible scenario, and I felt every possible emotion in your absence. I would be far too angry at you for putting me through so much distress if I didn't love you so much."

When she spotted her fan he still hadn't returned in the breast pocket of his dress coat, splayed out to reveal a lace similar to that of her gloves, a large smile spread across her face.

"I was taking care of Clara and settling a debt." He winked. "I'll act like I haven't seen you yet. Viscount's honor."

She laughed again as he kissed her other cheek and rushed through the open doors of the chapel. At least a hundred guests sat on either side of the aisle, each releasing audible breaths of relief at his arrival.

A burst of energy gave him what he needed to climb two more stairs to the dais where his friends stood as witnesses to the wedding on one side while Vivienne's friends and sisters stood on the other.

Barnaby approached, licked his finger, and Edward tried to unsuccessfully shove him away as he fixed his hair, and then next straightened his cravat, green to match Vivienne's dress.

"Did you even once look in the mirror this morning?" Barnaby accused as he fixed the lay of his sleeves next, and then re-fixed his hair when the previous fix didn't seem to appease him.

"It's been a busy day thus far," he admitted, his gaze flitting over the audience until he found Clara speaking animatedly to the duke on a back pew. He was shocked to find the duke allowing her to get more than just a single word in, as he was known for long-winded, one-sided conversations. And from how it appeared, he hung onto her every syllable, his eyes never leaving hers as if already smitten.

That, and after a failure to woo Vivienne, Edward wanted to believe the duke was trying harder to catch a wife by being more aware of his lengthy monologues.

He couldn't help but smile to see his sister happy, as well as to witness James' curiosity in the man as he peeked his head out from behind his mother. He hoped things went well for them. He truly did.

A musician struck up a slow, jovial song on the vielle, and nervous anticipation fluttered within his belly. But then his heart squeezed with fright as the entire room rumbled like an earthquake as the congregation stood for the bride when she appeared in the doorway on her father's arm.

His hand flew to his heart as it flipped and flopped within his chest from the scare. He felt silly as he lifted his pointed finger to Vivienne to signal he needed a moment while everyone's attention was fixed on her.

Bless the woman's heart, she turned right and left to show off her dress, the audience oohing and awing, while he focused on taking deep breaths and remaining on his feet. He would not have an episode on his wedding day. He *refused*.

Thankfully, his heart recovered. He straightened, and Vivienne then began to walk down the aisle with a large smile on her face. He couldn't help but mirror her happiness as he did, indeed, look at her as if he'd only seen her for the first time that morning.

He gazed at her with awe-filled eyes, admiring the way her skirts flowed around her with every step, the way her hair framed her lovely face, the way she exuded grace and poise with even the smallest movements.

This woman was going to be his *wife*. He still couldn't quite wrap his mind around it, as he was in a daze of disbelieving happiness.

Vivienne. His childhood friend. His sweetheart. The mother of his future child. He wanted to experience all of life's joys with her by his side.

Her father guided her hand into his and clasped them together beneath both of his, emotion surprisingly wavering in his eyes.

"You take good care of her," he murmured, emotion also thick in his throat. Vivienne would be the first to marry of all her siblings, and Edward supposed that giving her away likely was not easy.

"I will," he promised.

And then the warlord took a seat at the front of the chapel next to his brother—the king—and the rest of his family. But Edward couldn't divert his attention from Vivienne for long. His smile grew, the warmth in his heart burning him in the most pleasant way as he gazed into the rich brown of her eyes.

"You were right," she whispered.

"About what?"

"You looked at me as if you hadn't seen me already."

He chuckled and squeezed her hands. "I'm quite sure that's how I always look at you. I am rather smitten with you."

ADORINGLY, EDWARD

A beautiful, rosy blush filled her cheeks as the priestess began her short sermon. When she finished, he and Vivienne spoke their vows, to love and cherish and respect one another through sickness and through health.

Edward's heart pricked with emotion and immense gratitude when Vivienne gave a wholehearted "I do" to promise to love him even through sickness. His body was not strong. Perhaps it would never be. But for her to stay by his side through the thick and thin of it meant more to him than she could ever know.

They exchanged rings, and the priestess confirmed them husband and wife, instructing him to now kiss his bride.

Rather than a kiss, Vivienne threw her arms around his neck and held him tight as the audience clapped and whistled. And he couldn't help but return the embrace with a fierce, loving hold. He loved her more than anything in the entire world.

Finally, when they parted, he gently placed his hands on either side of her face and drew her in for a kiss. The audience cheered even louder, but all he could focus on was his beautiful, incredible wife as he kissed her once and then again, his heart full to bursting with love.

They had found each other again. And this time, he never planned to let her go.

Epilogue

TRUE TO DOCTOR CLARK'S word, Edward's health had improved exponentially over the next year and a half after his body had recovered from the arsenic poisoning. Of course, he still had his heart condition to contend with, but it was much more bearable than before, especially when the doctor administered a trial medicine that helped manage his heart and lungs.

Vivienne smiled joyfully as she and Edward walked along the bank of the river beneath the warm sunshine of late summer, each holding one of their daughter's tiny hands as she ambled forward on unsteady feet.

Elsie had gone nearly two weeks past her *actual* due date, that only she, her mother, and Edward had been privy to, and everyone thought she had been born over a month early. It was a good thing she had been small. Otherwise, people might have suspected the truth about her.

But Vivienne was quite happy with her little family of three that should someone accidentally learn of the truth, she knew it wouldn't break her. Wouldn't break *them*.

She smiled softly as her free hand rested over her still-flat belly as she amended her thoughts. Family of *four*. Not three. And Edward still had no idea.

"Up we go," Edward said with an overexaggerated grunt as they swung Elsie in the air between them. The small child squealed with laughter.

But the jarring movement struck Vivienne with nausea unlike any other, and her smile quickly fell into a distressed frown. She dropped Elsie's hand and rushed to the side of the path, fell to her hands and knees, and retched into the bushes.

She could have sobbed at the misery of vomiting, at the twisting and churning of her stomach until she was left with nothing but an immense soreness in her belly. She certainly hadn't missed this part of her last pregnancy, and she had almost forgotten of it until this one.

"Vivi!" Edward gasped as he appeared at her side, took her elbow, and helped her to unsteady feet. "Are you all right?" He brushed a strand of hair away from her mouth but then straightened suddenly, his eyes widening. "Are you with child?"

"It was supposed to be a surprise," she pouted as she held her hand over her stomach, trying not to retch for a second time.

Surprisingly, Edward laughed and spun her around in his arms, which did *not* help her queasy stomach. "You have to get better at hiding it if you want to keep it a surprise."

"Put me down, Edward! I'm going to vomit on you!"

He still laughed joyfully as he set her back down on her feet and pulled her into an embrace, holding her in a gentle manner as if to keep from pressing against her queasy belly. "I had no idea. This is still a wonderful surprise." And then he kissed the top of her head. "I quite remember you retching with Elsie as well. I was clueless then. Not so much now."

"Right out your window, too," she giggled but then regretted it when her stomach heaved, and she barely kept the remaining bile down. "It's any wonder you didn't catch on immediately."

When Elsie teetered a little too close to the riverbank, Edward released Vivienne and scooped Elsie into his arms, who shrieked with laughter and grabbed onto his hair. He continued to insist it really wasn't that long. But it was long enough for the child to grab ahold of it.

A soft smile lifted on her lips as she watched the two of them smile and giggle with one another. Edward was such a good father. He played with Elsie, read to her, droned on about the stars when she was nursing, and he often tucked her into bed each night.

"Did you hear that, Elsie?" Edward said as he held her little hand and placed it over Vivienne's belly. "You are going to be a big sister. Isn't that exciting?"

Elsie squealed and flapped her arms, reaching excitedly for her mother. Vivienne snatched her and planted kisses all across her face as she laughed some more.

And then Edward wrapped his arms around the both of them, keeping them safe and loved within his embrace.

Edward had been the best choice she had ever made. She knew she would always feel grateful for her decision to marry him, always cherish his unconditional love for both of them and the child on the way.

He, Elsie, and their unborn child were her everything. And she wouldn't change anything for the world.

ABOUT THE AUTHOR

Sydney Winward is an award-winning fantasy and paranormal romance author who dabbles in the occasional historical fiction. She loves building complex worlds filled with magic, strong characters, and emotional stories that can make you laugh and cry.

Sydney is the author of the Sunlight and Shadows Series and the best-selling Bloodborn Series, and when she's not writing, she's reading, thinking about stories, or going on adventures with her children. She lives in Utah with her husband and three amazing kids.

www.sydneywinward.com

www.ingramcontent.com/pod-product-compliance
Ingram Content Group UK Ltd.
Pitfield, Milton Keynes, MK11 3LW, UK
UKHW040909260225
455598UK00004B/127